I0588843

Dedicated to my sons,
Edwin and Owen,
who explore the Maine coast with me.

Ms Mia

and

Murder

on

Moose Isle

The Moose Isle Inn

Jennifer Branch

Ms. Mia and Murder on Moose Isle
Copyright © 2025 by Jennifer Branch Luallen
Registration Number: TXu002449834

All rights reserved. No part of this book may be
reproduced, scanned, or distributed in any printed or
electronic form without permission. Please do not
participate in or encourage piracy of copyrighted
materials in violation of the author's rights. Purchase
only authorized editions.

Published by BranchStudio LLC
Branchstudio.com

This book is a work of fiction. Names, characters,
places, and incidents either are products of the author's
imagination or are used fictitiously. Any resemblance
to actual persons, living or dead, events, or locales is
entirely coincidental.

Cover Design and Illustrations by Jennifer Branch.

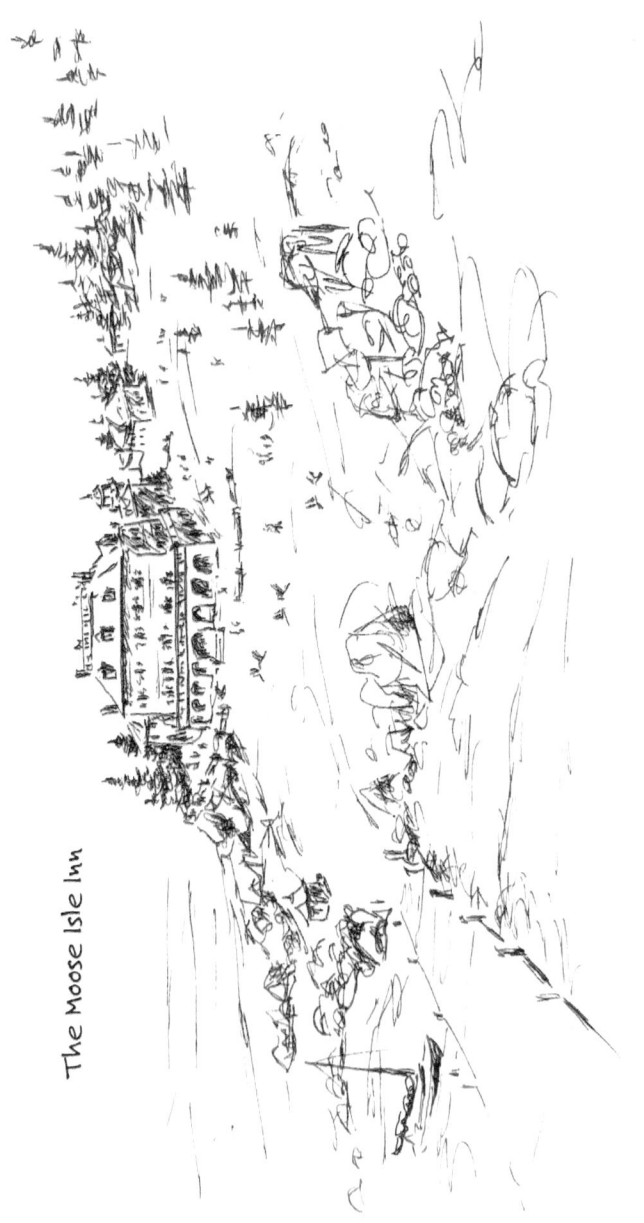

The Moose Isle Inn

This Changes Everything

Lauren Tisserande Baker raised her voice over the shocked cries, "Quiet, please."

The room hushed. With one short sentence she'd changed their lives and their company completely. "Tisserande Linens is moving all production back to the United States." Every single person in the room waited anxiously to hear more.

"For a long time, I've watched our town of Megeso Point, Maine, slowly dying. I've seen the thriving town my great-grandparents and you built fade away. Buildings stand vacant, stores close. Young people leave as soon as they graduate from high school. There are no jobs to keep them here, even if they wanted to stay. I want the town I grew up—we grew up in—to be more than just an empty shell."

Lauren looked around the company cafeteria. She knew every expectant face, from summer interns to veterans of fifty years. Her hands clenched the old oak podium her grandfather had made from scrap wood, until her knuckles hurt. If she didn't make the right decisions this time, the town she loved would never recover. They trusted her. She'd never been more scared—or more determined—in her life.

Roughly clearing her throat, she dove in. "I've felt for a while the current success of Tisserande Linens, my family's company, was bought by this town's empty storefronts. I know grandparents who never see their grandchildren. Their children left here because there were no jobs. We sent those jobs offshore." Lauren choked back tears. "We sold out so we could compete with the big box stores, where price always triumphs over quality. That can't be the only way. That shouldn't be our future."

She shook her head vehemently and risked a look at the small line of management flanking her. Most of the people surrounding her frankly disapproved of her risking their well-paid jobs to rehire people laid off a decade ago. They didn't understand that Lauren thought of every single person in the company, in the town, as her extended family. Most of them weren't from around here, but she'd grown up here. She'd baked cookies with their moms after school, ridden bikes on adventures, hauled lobster traps and picked apples with the people in this room. Megeso Point was her home.

Cynthia Clark, her VP of finance, tapped her pen sharply, punctuating her displeasure. Her strident voice echoed in Lauren's mind, "You'll end up ruining what's left of Tisserande. Then no one at all will have a job here." Well, she was risking it all, then.

"All that is changing right now, on my watch." She spoke forcefully. "We're bringing back quality, made in the USA, made in Maine, made by us in our great town. We're rebuilding our town and our company like it should be. We're rebuilding with jobs first."

The room cheered and feet stomped wildly.

Lauren spoke over the thunderous approval. "It's not going to happen overnight, but we're doing this as fast as possible." She was gambling all Tisserande's profits, as well as most of her own capital, on the expansion. Working fast took money and lots of it.

The room stilled again. No one wanted to miss a word.

"I've devised a five-year plan to bring all production back to the United States, starting with a new high-end line. In two weeks, we break ground on a state of the art production facility that will provide work for an additional two hundred employees in Megeso Point by next year. That's just the start." Lauren nodded at the VP of Production, Max Davis, who gave her a quick, approving smile. "Max is already building the machines for the new line." She grinned suddenly. "That's the complicated mess in his workshop you've all been asking about. "

The room laughed a little, with relief more than mirth.

She continued, gripping the podium so hard her knuckles turned white, "The next phase will move the rest of our offshore production back home, creating more jobs for the community. With modern engineering capabilities, we can keep all of our production in-house, and improve the quality dramatically at the same time."

On her right, her husband, Paul Baker, the company president, muttered sourly, "And lower the profit tremendously." He crossed his arms tightly, distancing himself from the announcement.

Ignoring him, she raised her voice. "We can make our community thrive again, and build Tisserande Linens into a better company."

"What about the old factory?" someone shouted from the back of the cafeteria.

"We have plans to refurbish it into a store," Lauren told them. "We can use it for a seconds outlet, like we used to have."

"People would drive all the way from Boston to shop," Cynthia commented grudgingly. "It brought a nice profit, from what I understand." Her pen tapping slowed slightly.

"Where's the new factory going?" a gawky kid yelled out, raising his hand, as if in school. He didn't look like he was old enough to be out of school.

"The old Malone estate, right behind the old factory. It went up for sale, zoned industrial. We're closing on it next week," Lauren said proudly. It had been the perfect location, just outside the town center. Not too far to drive during the brutal Maine winters. Not a potential eyesore in the middle of town.

"That old house was falling apart, even before the

fire."

"Sure was."

Her husband grumbled, "It costs enough, even then." He looked down at the crowd with disgust.

"You hiring for construction?" a woman's voice rang out.

Lauren assured them, "Part of the construction agreement is they hire as much as they can locally. The factory is modular, so we can get started quickly and add to it as we go."

An excited chatter arose from everyone who had a cousin or uncle in the building industry.

Lauren said loudly, over the noise, "A whole new chapter is starting at Tisserande Linens and Megeso Point. Together, we're going to make our linens, our company and our town better than ever." She grinned, thinking of high school, and yelled, "Go Eagles!"

A huge cry went up, echoing her with their school cheer. Lauren felt tears in her eyes. Her husband looked at her, smirking at the effect the cheering had on her. She glared at him quickly, then glanced away. The factory build was out of his hands now. She knew she was doing the right thing, both for her and her hometown.

As the cheers died down, Lauren closed the meeting. "In the back of the room, besides doughnuts and coffee, we have a scale model and sketches of the new facility, so you can see where we'll be working next year."

With a flourish, the sheet was pulled off the model and people crowded around. The room roared with the excitement of the crowd realizing their town could thrive again.

2

Hotel Arrivals

Mia Spinel relaxed in one of the Adirondack chairs dotting the smooth green grass and looked out across the rich blue of the Atlantic Ocean.

It was a glorious day, with just enough chill in the air to give her a reason for a cozy pink cashmere sweater and her cup of mulled cider. She'd walked around Moose Isle Inn that afternoon, exploring the hotel grounds thoroughly.

Now, with her pink tennis shoes propped on the footrest, Mia gazed out at the breathtaking view spread before her. Moose Isle, a granite island emerging from the bay, was just tall enough to give a good view from almost anywhere. The inn stood proudly at the top.

The Spinel Moose Isle Inn was a grand Gilded Age relic, a huge white clapboard building stretching up three stories, topped by a slate roof and a glassed-in widow's walk. You could almost see the core of the house, even now, but large additions from ballrooms to guest rooms had sprouted from the main shell over the years. Lush green lawn, in defiance of the scanty Maine soil, carpeted the stretch between the main building and the shore, dotted with strategically placed balsam fir windbreaks.

On this side of the island, rocky cliffs stood high, guarding the island from the winter rage of the sea. The cliff tops were edged with pink beach roses, their scent mixing with salty iodine. The other side of the island sloped to a rocky beach full of pink granite balls. The hardy could swim in the chilly water in high summer, but the neighboring boat dock and fishing pier were more popular destinations. Most people preferred the glass-enclosed heated pool off the hotel for actual swimming.

The hotel manager, Joseph Curry, casually strolled up, elegant as always in a Harris tweed jacket and wool trousers. "Enjoying your cider, Ms. Mia?"

Mia sipped the hot cider, inhaling the scent of rich apples and spices.

"It's wonderful, Joseph. Everything looks great here."

"I'm glad. I never know what you'll tell me to fix on your first day here," he said sardonically. He sat in the neighboring chair and propped his feet up. Mia noticed his socks had tiny red lobsters decorating them, coordinating perfectly with a faint red line in his tweed jacket.

Joseph still cultivated a faint English accent, even after many years in the United States. Mia always found it amusing that the sophisticated man had chosen one of their more rustic hotels. He'd turned it into the Gilded Age splendor it was, a refined haven marooned on a wild Maine island. He'd definitely borrowed from that bygone era's rusticators' mentality. The hotel offered glorious daytime nature excursions around the island (always with appetizing picnic baskets in tow) followed by dinners worth waiting for. The winning combination drew guests, and kept them returning year after year.

"I know we have close to a full house," Mia said. Joseph nodded serene agreement. "But what guests do we have this week?"

"Only one wedding this weekend. It's still early in the season, but the bride wants a spring wedding," Joseph told her, his long, narrow face thoughtfully considering weekend plans. "It's a small affair, just thirty guests. Mostly family."

"I shouldn't say it as a hotel owner, but I think the more intimate weddings are usually the most fun."

"They're certainly the easiest to manage and keep everyone happy. This hotel definitely encourages the smaller weddings, with only sixty rooms." He waved his long fingers to encompass the hotel. "Lots of interesting activities for different age groups too. Hiking for the kids and elderly grandmothers can sit and watch the ocean." He smiled meaningfully at Mia.

Mia grinned back in mock disdain. "I'm not a grandma yet, thank you." She patted her smooth blonde hair. Not a gray hair showed—they wouldn't dare.

"Just a matter of time," he teased her, bony

shoulders shaking in silent laughter.

Mia ignored him, looking out at the water. A new group seemed to be arriving.

"It makes for an exciting adventure, arriving on the boat. There's just something about an island." She loved watching new guests arriving. The Moose Isle Inn used a gorgeous Hinckley Picnic Boat for one of their hotel ferries. Wood and brass glowed in the orange tinged afternoon sun. The design was an elegant refinement of a lobster boat, riding all seas with graceful ease.

A woman lounged in the stern, arm draped casually across the back of the navy blue striped cushion, large dark sunglasses turned toward the setting sun, an excited smile on her face. A dark haired man sat across from her, laughing at something she'd said. On her other side, another man perched stiffly, not letting his body relax into the roll of the waves. A young woman clutched his arm, her spun-sugar blonde hair spilling onto his jacket. Mia could almost hear her squeal as she jumped and clung to the older man whenever the spray might possibly touch her.

"Ah, the weekend's company junket has arrived," Joseph Curry told her. "The management of Tisserande Linens. You know, they used to make the best towels and sheets in the Northeast."

"It looks like a good group," Mia said. She peered with interest at the new arrivals. She'd have to get some bird watching binoculars to tuck in her bag. They would be so handy for closer observation. Only of birds, of course.

"The management is having their annual get together to congratulate themselves on record profits again, I'm assuming. A very successful company." He frowned, "It's rather odd they're coming here, you know. The factory, well, just the company headquarters now, is up the coast a little, in Megeso Point. It's only a few towns away. I think they usually head to the Caribbean or somewhere."

"May in the Caribbean is beginning to heat up," Mia said. "It's much more pleasant weather here now."

"Yes, but I think winter is their usual time for their company affair. Winter's a better time to get away, around here. Who wants to wade through snow instead of walk on a sunny beach?" His face turned sharp, like a terrier on the scent. "I wonder why they're here now."

Mia smiled at his interest, "I expect we'll know by the end of the weekend."

"I expect we will." Joseph watched the group disembarking with focused attention.

As the boat docked, three men ducked out from the open cabin, two with drinks in hand. Douglas, the hotel harbor master, scowled at them, firmly removing their cut crystal glasses after they'd gulped the dregs.

Arriving in the boat was a perfect start to their stay, Mia thought, as she saw the happy face of the young woman tenderly helped off the boat by the man next to her. He smiled down at her, while helping the next passenger disembark safely. The woman laughed in delight as she pointed to one of the little sailboats ready for guests' use. He nodded enthusiastically, the two clearly planning a weekend sail.

The woman strode easily up the gentle slope of the island, leaving the group to follow her. Her wide pants rippled in the breeze, and her green sweater clung to her trim body. She moved like an athlete, long graceful strides making an easy journey up the hill. Laughing in pure joy, she pointed back to the mainland, Cadillac Mountain's pink granite glowing in the setting sun. "Isn't it beautiful?" she told Mia and anyone in earshot.

She paused to gather her group at the main entrance of the hotel. Only one other woman had kept up with her, the rest straggled behind.

The pale blonde woman's high heels caught on the rocks, making for awkward progress as she clung to the older man's arm. She apparently didn't think much of the rustic setting of the hotel, looking around her with disbelief. Her shocked, high pitched voice squeaked, "There's really nowhere to shop on the island? Why would anyone come here?"

The man informed her, "Oh, I think there are a few local shops in the village. Very arts and crafty."

The young woman made a face. "Not exactly my style, darling. Why couldn't we go to New York again this year? We live in Maine. Why do we have to vacation in this hell hole too?" Her perfectly fitted dressy pants suit, shiny silk blouse and expertly applied makeup agreed. The two continued their stilted progress up the rocky hill.

A woman with streaked spiky hair and orange framed glasses trudged by next. She was a little out of breath with a reddened face, even on the gentle slope. Her heron thin legs, clad in unfortunate orange pants, struggled to scale the hill, every joint clearly protesting her unusual spurt of activity.

Two men, who thought they were younger than they were, raced up to the hotel. Neither came out of it with flying colors. They collapsed on the green lawn in laughter, still breathing hard, as if running to the hotel was the funniest thing in the world.

A gawky man with big glasses lagged behind them, not joining in the race. He gazed around him with happy wonder, smiling at the hotel and waving a cheerful goodbye to the boat captain, who completely ignored him. He walked leisurely up the hill, stopping to admire his surroundings every other step, completely unconcerned about catching up with the others.

Very last to emerge from deep in the boat's interior was a well padded blonde in shiny candy-pink with bright heels to match and a bloated whale of a man. He heaved himself out of the cabin, balancing carefully on the deck, his flesh quivering as he caught his balance. Wobbling, he cautiously stepped onto the dock, the boat rebounding visibly as it was relieved of his weight. He began his measured tread down the center of the dock, not bothering to look back at his companion.

The woman in pink waited a minute, clearly expecting the boat captain to help her on to the dock. He completely ignored her, ducking below.

Mia smiled a little, wondering how long it would

take the woman to realize Douglas was not coming back on deck while he was alone with a woman on his boat.

Finally realizing the only way off the boat was on her own, she eased herself to the edge and jumped off, hampered only slightly by her spike heels. She lumbered up the hill, trying to catch up to the rest of the party.

Mia saw Douglas pop his head out of belowdecks, like a groundhog checking for safety. When he confirmed the passengers were well and truly off his boat, he ventured out with an obvious look of relief, making Mia smile.

The hotel concierge, a petite blonde vibrating with energy, came out to greet the scattered group. She expertly herded them, holding the door to encourage them to come inside. A bellboy hurried down the hill with a cart to gather the luggage Douglas was grudgingly offloading.

Joseph laughed softly after the little group entered the hotel. "That looks like a fun little junket. I'm glad I'm not the one trying to make them work together."

"Me too," Mia said, laughing. "I doubt they ever agree on anything. And I can't believe those two overaged boys ever work."

"I also agree with that young woman. This island is not exactly her style. New York would suit her much better."

"She's certainly not here by choice," Mia observed. "So that's the Tisserande group. Who else is

14

here?"

"Mostly couples having romantic getaways. A few foodies making their pilgrimage to the fabulous Chef Ava. One or two family groups. Nothing out of the ordinary."

"That sounds like a good mix," Mia got up and stretched her arms out. "This island is always so relaxing."

She motioned to a happy older couple, a table between them heaped high with a glorious afternoon tea. The rotund man spread blueberry jam on a golden popover with gusto, his face avidly anticipating the treat. "Your teas always look as delicious as they taste. It makes me feel like being lazy."

"You were climbing up and down cliffs all morning," Joseph reminded her. "I'm not surprised you're hungry." He pursed his lips. "You know Mark will kill me if you break an ankle. It's not just your life you're risking."

Mark Spinel, one of Mia's two stepsons, would definitely know who to blame if Mia broke something climbing on rocks. He'd blame Mia and berate her unmercifully, as usual. Not that it made a bit of difference.

Her stepsons and daughter adored Mia, but they much preferred her spending her energy organizing the Spinel family's hotels around the world, rather than home in Atlanta, organizing their personal lives. They actively encouraged Mia to travel as much as possible—and send back interesting presents.

"I'm looking forward to visiting the town

15

tomorrow." The town proper was on the opposite end of the island from the hotel, a short brisk walk away. "Right now, I'm going to dress for dinner, and enjoy the hotel for a few minutes."

"Wonderful. I will see you later, then." Joseph made no move to go, gazing out to sea at the passing sailboats with calm interest, his long legs neatly crossed, polished leather brogues gently waving to his inner music.

Mia had never caught Joseph Curry doing any work whatsoever. He wandered around the hotel, gently gossiping, his elegantly lean body moving languidly, with all the time in the world at his disposal. She'd never actually spotted him in his wood paneled office. Sometimes there were recent signs he'd been there, an open laptop, papers on the ornate antique desk, a still warm coffee cup. Never the actual man sitting in his office, doing anything as mundane as working. Joseph was strolling through the hotel, leisurely chatting with everyone. Nothing happened on the island without him knowing about it.

He was also one of the most efficient managers Spinel Hotels had. Joseph had organized several of their hotels around the world, and finally settled down here, on Moose Isle, when they'd first bought the property.

The hotel had been a decrepit, once grand house that had housed everything from a wartime convalescent hospital to a cult headquarters in its day. The only thing going for the aged wreck of an obsolete house when they'd first seen it was its sublime location

16

in the Cranberry Islands of Maine, just off Mount Desert Island, with breathtaking views of Acadia National Park.

Mia and her late husband, Leo Spinel, had helped organize the complete renovation of the Gilded Age summer vacation "cottage." The beautiful structure of the immense white house was rescued, while the necessary ingredients for a luxury destination resort, such as the spa, meeting rooms and excellent bathrooms in every room, were added. Luckily, the original extravagant owners had planned their summer home to hold all of their hundred nearest and dearest in spacious rooms, so sixty guest rooms had easily been carved out of the hulk, with a few discrete additions.

Joseph had taken charge of the renovation. A magnificent hotel, like stepping back into another era, rose from the ruins. He'd flatly refused to take on any new projects, preferring to stay with his grand creation in rustic Maine. He lived in a charming cottage, designed by himself, on the hotel grounds, and seldom left his beloved island.

Mia loved coming here for two weeks a year, before the true Maine summer season started. She might suggest a few things to improve the hotel during her visit, but most of her time was spent simply enjoying the wonderful island and the season. Joseph always had the hotel in perfect order. She was on vacation.

The wide front porch held old fashioned white wicker chairs adorned with bright floral cushions and a view of the surrounding islands. An elderly lady with a froth of snow white hair and smile of eager anticipation perched, eying the silver tea tray placed on a table in front of her. A plate of blueberry scones waited temptingly, just in reach. Visibly giving in to an internal struggle, she smiled up at Mia, placing one on her plate, "I think I'd better get mine before my grandchildren get here. They've been hiking all day, and I think these delicious looking scones will disappear quickly."

"Absolutely." Mia remembered how fast dinner disappeared as soon as hungry children sat down.

The dark wood paneled hall inside was designed for grand entrances, with a curved staircase on either side of the large hallway leading into the main lobby. A chandelier dripped sparkling crystals from the ceiling, but most of the lighting was discretely ambient. She nodded in greeting to Kayla, the concierge, who immediately jumped up to see if she could possibly help Mia with anything.

"Can you make a reservation for tonight in the Acadia Dining Room?"

"I'll tell Chef Ava," Kayla said, bouncing with enthusiasm. "You have to try her clam chowdah. It's better than my mom's."

"I wouldn't tell your mom that. She might not make it for you any more," Mia told her with a smile, looking around the hall. "There aren't many people in the lobby right now?"

"Oh, everyone goes to the library, Ms. Mia. That's where we set out the nibbles." She consulted the huge grandfather clock ensconced in the corner. "People will start gathering there in about an hour."

"Thanks, Kayla. I'll just go and change for dinner, then." Mia headed for the elevators, surreptitiously tucked behind the grand stairway.

Her room was in the main building, one of the large older rooms surviving with its beautiful proportions intact. Her bathroom was carved off from the neighboring room. There were only two true suites at the Moose Isle Inn, with most of the large rooms arranged, like Mia's, into distinct bedroom and living room spaces.

The room felt airy and bright, with creamy white paneled walls catching the warm sunlight. Tall French doors led to a balcony just big enough for two chairs and a tiny table, but with a magnificent view of the coast. A massive antique bed sat majestically on one side of the room, pale blue curtained drapes framing the tall four poster. Across the large room, a blue and gold Persian rug framed a sofa and two comfortable chairs pulled up to a tall fireplace. An exquisite watercolor of Cadillac Mountain held pride of place above the fireplace. A little sign hung next to it, "Pull for Fire Service," with an old fashioned twisted pull rope beside it. Mia immediately planned at least one evening with a cheerful fire and a good book.

A bottle of champagne and a small cheese board waited for her on the coffee table. She smiled at Joseph's thoughtfulness and poured a glass of perfectly chilled champagne. Sipping, she nibbled cheese and a cracker and walked to the balcony, leaning on the railing.

From the balcony, she saw the whole of Southwest Harbor in the distance. A lobster boat piled high with traps was headed out to sea. A beautiful wooden yawl, sails folded in the calm evening air, returned to the harbor after a day spent sailing the Maine summer sea. Tiny lights showed along Mount Desert Island's coast, with just an occasional house light up higher on the mountains. She tried to remember what the town in the near distance was— maybe Northeast Harbor?

She remembered going to this house long ago with her husband, Leo, wondering if they could possibly make it into a hotel. The short boat ride here had been miserable, gray and choppy. They hadn't been able to climb the stairs to the third floor, so many of the boards had been missing. They'd explored the property, planning together, deciding whether the tattered remnant was worth making into a hotel.

Leo hadn't been bald then. She smiled in fond remembrance of his windblown hair standing straight up. He'd looked like a mischievous round faced elf. She still missed him every day, even after two years. They'd had a wonderful life together. After the children were grown, they'd explored the world, living at all the Spinel Hotels in turn. They'd spend a few weeks or a few months perfecting each hotel, then move on to the next.

Mia tried to keep that spirit of adventure they'd enjoyed together. Even now she traveled on her own, she saw each new day as a precious gift to open. After all, you never knew what wonderful things the next day might bring.

The Moose Isle Inn had turned out even better than they'd expected, on that long ago windswept morning. Joseph deserved the credit for its transformation into a premier destination. And Chef Ava—her dinners were fabulous. Looking forward to tonight, Mia thought Moose Isle Inn was truly a hotel to savor. She sighed in pleasure, then suddenly sniffed sharply.

She definitely smelled smoke. Leaning out, she didn't see any bonfires on the grounds, but she did see smoke coming from a balcony at the other end of the wing. Mia quickly called Kayla, then hurried down the hall. One door had smoke oozing out from under the door frame. She knocked hard. "Is anyone in there? Is everything okay?"

A faint voice called back, "Everything's fine, just fine."

"There's smoke coming out of your room. You need to open this door right now." Several of the hospitality team ran up brandishing fire extinguishers, followed by Joseph strolling behind, massive red fire extinguisher casually swinging at his side. Even with modern fire prevention installed, fire was taken very seriously on an isolated island.

"Just a minute," and sounds of frantic activity behind the door. The door opened slowly and an innocent blue eye peeked out. "We're right in the middle of something. Can we get back to you?"

Mia demanded, "There is smoke billowing from your room. Open your door immediately."

The door opened to reveal a woman, graying hair pulled back in a disheveled ponytail, wearing an apron. "Smoke? We're not smoking salmon until tomorrow," she said, confused.

Mia pushed past her.

A man stood in front of a portable gas burner, frantically stirring a pan over the roaring blue flame in a cloud of smoke. "I am sorry, searing steaks always does create a tiny bit of smoke. I should have set up on the balcony. I'll remember that next time." His chubby face was shiny with sweat as he happily stirred. "I've almost got this finished and I'll turn it off. The smoke will be gone in a jiffy. So sorry to worry you."

Mia surveyed the room. This room had a mini fridge and bar accouterments built into one side of the room, designed for afternoon cocktails and keeping children's snacks cold. The occupants had taken these meager offerings and ran with them.

A four burner camping stove stood in pride of place, surrounded by small folding countertops, even a kitchen island with a wooden chopping block, grouped around the bar area. The man wore a huge apron with "Kiss the Chef" on it. Her apron was festooned with vegetables, from peas to carrots. Blissful smiles lit their faces, completely ignoring the smoke filling the room.

Mia glanced at Joseph. His face was carefully expressionless as he slowly swung the fire extinguisher like a pendulum.

"Hello, I'm Mia Spinel, one of the hotel owners."

The plump woman smiled in greeting. "Hi, nice to meet you. I'm Tina Michaud and that's my husband

22

Andrew manning the stove. I'm sous chef today." She took up a handful of fine green onions and chopped with professional speed.

"Ah," Mia watched the blurred knife for a minute.

Andrew Michaud poured the contents of his pan over the resting steaks with a flourish. "Chanterelles from the woods next to the shore. Lovely, aren't they?" He looked at them inquiringly, "If you don't mind, I'd like to eat this while it's perfection."

The delicious smell of mushrooms wafted toward Mia. Her stomach growled in answer.

"Chanterelles, picked this afternoon," Andrew said proudly. "You just can't beat that."

Joseph broke in forcefully, "I'm Joseph Curry, the hotel manager. You can't cook in your room like this."

Mia added, "No, you can't."

"But that's why we came," Andrew objected, taking off his apron. "Moose Isle is a chef's paradise. Chanterelles, wild blueberries and raspberries, lobster, mussels, salmon—I couldn't count the delicious edibles on this island. And that's only this season."

"But...," Joseph was clearly at a loss for once.

Mia was never at a loss. "You can't cook in your room." She held up her hands to their objection. "I completely understand your passion for cooking. How would a small corner of the restaurant kitchen work for you?"

They hesitated. "We've got all our equipment set up already," Andrew demurred.

They certainly did.

Mia repeated, "You can't cook in your room. It would completely void our insurance policy." Insurance was always a useful tactic for recalcitrant guests.

Tina Michaud exclaimed, "I didn't even think of that." Her face fell.

"You can use the hotel kitchen." Mia nodded encouragingly. "After you enjoy your wonderful dinner, the hospitality team will come by to pick up your," she gestured, "supplies and take them to the hotel kitchen. You won't have to do a thing." She needed to relocate their stove immediately.

Joseph cut in, "I would like to request you cook around the peak kitchen times so our hotel chefs aren't inconvenienced."

"Absolutely," Andrew agreed, gazing at his steak longingly.

"Then that's settled," Mia said with a smile. "Enjoy your dinner."

As they left, they heard Tina ask, "Can we still do Crêpes Suzette, do you think?"

Joseph started, then visibly decided to let it drop.

Mia smiled at him, opening her door. "Hotels are never boring, are they?"

"Not that I have found." He walked away, the huge fire extinguisher casually swinging by his side.

Mia laughed as she changed for dinner into a smooth green wool dress. The smell of Andrew and Tina's steaks had whetted her appetite. And she must be sure to have some chanterelles during her visit. The mushrooms were one of her favorite treats.

Approving of the large marble bathroom, she

planned a lovely soak that evening in the massive clawfoot tub centered on the window, discretely covered with filmy curtains. She sponged off the day's hike from her face, then applied her evening makeup, little touches of eyeliner and mascara to highlight her bright blue eyes and a cheerful pink lipstick as a finishing touch. She wound a creamy cashmere wrap around her, planning for the chill of a Maine early summer evening.

Two large green spinel earrings, ringed with tiny diamonds and a matching necklace completed her wardrobe. She remembered her husband's eager smile watching her unwrap the set. Leo Spinel always gave her spinel jewelry, because of their name. And every time she wore the green spinels, she could see him smiling at her. She smiled back at herself in the mirror, and sipped her champagne in happy anticipation of Chef Ava's dinner.

3

Starry Night

Stepping onto the balcony framing the library was an experience never forgotten. The library was the centerpiece of the hotel, and justly so. The huge octagonal room, three stories high, was capped by a widows walk at the very top, reached by a tiny circular stair. The vibrant colors of the books glowed with energy against panels of rich, dark wood. Airy constellations sprinkled with gold stars adorned the night sky blue, domed ceiling.

Books weren't merely an afterthought, as in most hotels, either. There were always the expected latest fiction and non-fiction in shiny new covers, but Joseph spent winter scouring the local bookstores and library sales for interesting additions to the massive collection. Anything catching his eye was added to the eclectic mix. He read them all first, of course. Shelves lined the first two floors, except for tall glass doors leading to the terrace. The windows around the widow's walk balcony let light stream in during the day, but they were dark now, screened by rich velvet draperies.

Mia leaned over the oak railing and looked down at the first floor. The intricately patterned Oriental rugs lay scattered across the huge room, creating conversation groupings. A fire roared in the massive stone fireplace, warming hearts as well as bodies. The room lay empty, with an air of anticipation of evening festivities. Approaching the intricately carved circular staircase, she grinned back at a lurking wooden gargoyle and carefully descended the narrow steps. After choosing the best vantage point for arrivals, she settled in a tall wing chair close to the fire and surveyed the room. Immediately, a waitress appeared like a genie from a bottle, "May I get you something before dinner, Ms. Mia?" she eagerly asked.

Mia thought of the wonderful tea she'd seen on the porch. "Thanks, Sydney. I'd love one of those blueberry scones I saw earlier and a glass of champagne."

"Yes, ma'am," the young waitress bustled away, her coltish legs moving with unexpected speed.

Mia looked around the ornate library, appreciating the fine details that had gone into its creation. The ceiling was even more dramatic seen from directly below, the clever lighting just at the edges of the dome made it seem much deeper than it really was. Golden stars twinkled in the blue depths, like a magical portal.

"Isn't it wonderful?" a woman's cheerful voice cut into Mia's reverie. She collapsed into a neighboring wing chair and gazed up in pleasure. "It's an absolutely gorgeous hotel. And these books," she gestured at the wealth of books. "Usually, hotels just buy matching sets of books by the yard, plus the latest bestsellers. So boring. All for the look of the thing, not to actually read. I just saw a book on Ming Dynasty porcelain next to one on the Dead Sea Scrolls. And a sort of encyclopedia of seaweed. It's the kind of library you dream of having on long winter nights. It'll take me forever to decide on my evening book." She looked around her with clear satisfaction, flipping her glossy hair back against her shoulders.

Sydney placed a silver tray with a large plate of scones on the little table between the women and the newcomer's smile broadened. "Blueberry scones! It just gets better and better."

"I know," Mia took a scone and sipped her chilled champagne. "It's the perfect tea party." She raised her glass, "but made even better with champagne."

"A Collet Brut Art Deco, Ms. Mia," the waitress informed her. "Mr. Jackson remembered you enjoying it on your last visit."

"Excellent choice." Mia sipped again, enjoying the chill of the golden bubbles on her tongue.

"I think I'll have one of those, too. I feel like celebrating tonight," the woman told the waitress, obviously reading the name tag. "Thanks, Sydney." She leaned back with her scone. Her athletic frame was set off with a well cut dark dress of the sort suitable for a range of occasions, from weddings to funerals to a nice night out at a fine restaurant. She had a substantial, but not overlarge for everyday wear, diamond engagement set and three carat sparkling diamond stud earrings, all the overt trappings of a well bred and well heeled New England native.

Her accent marked her as a Downeast Mainer, "You know, I grew up not too far from here. I've lived in the area all my life, but I've never been here before. Everyone always says it's wonderful, but I just didn't get around to it. I can't believe what I've been missing." She took a happy bite of her scone. "So, so good."

"You probably go further for vacation, since you live in this beautiful area already."

"Yes, but this is such a nice weekend getaway. I can't believe I've never stayed here before." She looked around the room appreciatively.

"There's always time to start something new."

"I know." The young woman smiled mischievously, obviously dying to tell someone what she'd been up to. "I've just turned my company, Tisserande Linens, completely upside down. A decade or so ago, the company started sending all the manufacturing offshore." She shrugged off the excuse. "I get it, it was a lot cheaper and everyone was just interested in cheap stuff then, not quality. You can't exactly compete in the big-box stores without cheap prices."

"I hope that's swinging the other way," Mia said.

"I think people are appreciating good quality again."

"I certainly hope so." Her long fingers picked at the silky wool of her dress, then smoothed it back into place. "I've just bet my company on it. I'm building a state-of-the-art factory next to the old one we closed, and moving production back home."

"That's a huge step," Mia encouraged.

"I know." She nervously stroked her long dark hair, resettling the gold clip. "I just couldn't watch my hometown dying any more without doing something about it." She laughed, "And, you know, after I'd seen the latest samples from the offshore factory, I got out my great grandmother's sheets and compared them. They were some of the first the Tisserande factory produced in the United States, and still so wonderfully strong and smooth. It's sad we can't find that quality at the store anymore. So, I decided to remake it, like we had then."

She leaned forward, green eyes dancing with excitement. "We still have some of the very same equipment those were made on. My engineer has worked out how to replicate those smooth crisp sheets I remember from my childhood, hybridizing old and new equipment — making it safer and more efficient."

"That's so exciting," Mia leaned forward too. She appreciated quality and loved other people taking the time to as well.

"I know." Lauren perched on the edge of her chair. "We're going to make everything here, in the USA. We're buying organic cotton from South Carolina, processing it down there, but making the sheets at home in Maine, just like we used to do. We'll not only give back to our community; we'll be able to control every aspect of the process ourselves." She held up her hands, laughing at herself. "You wouldn't believe how much difference the fiber length and the thread size make. I've been really nerding out about the whole process. Don't even get me started on towels. Or how different dyes affect the fabric."

"I can believe it." Mia told her, smiling at the young woman's excitement. "It's almost impossible to find good sheets or towels."

She leaned in toward Mia, "You know, one of the reasons I wanted to come here besides needing a quick break before the upcoming project—we usually do a package deal in the Caribbean during winter—is I wanted to see what luxury hotel sheets were like before I finalized ours." She laughed at herself. "Silly, huh?" She shook her head at her absurd idea. "They were pretty much our highest quality sheets. Not our brand, but about the same quality. Good for a while. I doubt they last longer than a season here or a year in someone's home. I'd like to speak to the owner when we get our factory in production. Show them what luxury sheets really feel like."

Mia grinned. It was too good an opportunity. "Let me introduce myself. I'm Mia Spinel, one of the hotel owners."

The woman's mouth dropped open, but she recovered quickly. "Well, you know I'm a Tisserande. I'm Lauren Tisserande Baker." She shook her head in disbelief, "I can't believe you're Mrs. Spinel. I was wondering earlier about asking the manager for an introduction to the owners, when we had our factory up and running."

"Just call me Mia, dear." She smiled reassuringly. "When will the United States factory be running?"

"Within a year. I'm closing next week on the property, and I have the builders lined up, ready to start work that day."

"That's quick work."

"Well, my production engineer, Max, and I have been planning this carefully. I don't have full control of my company until my birthday this weekend—this trip is partly my birthday party." She giggled a little, happy at the treat.

"Happy Birthday, Lauren," Mia mentally planned for a birthday cake to be presented at one dinner during Lauren's stay.

"There's such a short season to build in Maine that the building itself has to be finished by September, so everything had to be preordered and planned. Just a few months to get the shell done. We can't pour concrete on frozen ground or work in snow. Once the exterior is finished, there's less of a rush, but I want things moving as quickly as possible." Lauren vibrated with energy, spilling out in her words.

"I can tell." The woman's enthusiasm was infectious.

"I grew up in Megeso Point. It's my home. The factory's empty now. We just have a corporate headquarters and distribution center." She shook her head sadly, "I look at all those empty stores along Main

33

Street now, and it makes me just want to cry." Her strong hands clenched and unclenched on the material of her dress. "I feel like the town's just going away, a little every day."

Mia nodded, "I know what you mean. It's the saddest thing in the world when a community dies." She'd seen too many small towns die from lack of jobs. No wonder Lauren was in a hurry to build her factory.

"Once there are jobs, the town will rejuvenate quickly, I think," Lauren said hopefully. "It's an absolutely beautiful place to live. I want jobs available for the next round of high school graduates. The town needs young people staying home, not being forced to leave town to find jobs after graduation. And we need our college graduates returning home to jobs. The young people can't stay, no matter how much they might want to, if there's no work." Lauren smiled at Mia as several people from her group walked into the room, "I think people are ready for really good quality linens again too."

"I certainly am," Mia said, with feeling, remembering the last bedding samples she'd been shown. "Call me directly when you're ready to start selling. If they're as good as you've planned, Spinel Hotels will be your very first customer." There was nothing Mia liked better than a good cause merging with high quality.

"That's wonderful," Lauren smiled wholeheartedly at approaching newcomers, and held up her hand to motion them over. "I think everything's falling into place like it's meant to be, isn't it, honey?"

She greeted the tall man at the front with a welcoming hand resting lightly on his arm. His once athletic frame was running to fat with the beginnings of a spare tire. Sun wrinkles grooved his face, but a cocky grin and a devil may care air made him quite attractive, still. "This is my husband, Paul Baker, Tisserande's CEO. Paul, this is Mia Spinel, one of the hotel owners."

Mia saw his smile twitch brighter as he understood she was one of the hotel Spinels. "Nice to meet you, Mia." He shook her hand heartily, slipping into salesman mode with ease. "Quite a little place you have here," he laughed at the understatement. "Must be hell to maintain it in these Maine winters we get."

"It's nice to meet you, Paul," Mia told him. "Lauren has been telling me of your company's wonderful future plans."

"Yeah, well," he said dismissively, smoothing his sun streaked hair. "That's all Lauren. I'm all for sticking with the factories I've been working with. We know they can deliver at the right price."

Lauren's smile grew a little fixed. "Mia's interested in our new luxury line, honey," ending the sentence with a purposeful emphasis.

"Yeah, yeah," he smiled winningly at Mia. "But you've got to balance luxury and cost with so many hotels, don't you? You don't want to just throw money away on something guests won't even notice. Past a certain level, what's it matter? No one's going to notice but your bottom line."

Mia said tightly, "I never compromise on quality.

We always get the very best we can find. Don't you think that's the right attitude, Lauren?"

"I do," Lauren said awkwardly. Her feet shifted, toes pointing inward. "Like these scones—they're absolutely delicious. Try one, Paul."

"Yum," he said after a bite wolfing down half the scone in a gulp. "Yeah, those are wicked good." He crammed the rest in his mouth. Mia tried not to look.

Lauren filled the awkward gap. "I know they're Maine blueberries, but how does the chef get them so buttery and flaky at the same time? Mine never turn out like that."

"You haven't had much practice, dear," Paul pointed out in a cutting note. "Cooking isn't exactly your strong suit." He grabbed another scone.

Lauren shrugged off the remark with an embarrassed smile. "I know it isn't, but I keep trying. My scones turn out okay, but not like this, do they, Max?"

A raven haired athletic man, with a wind etched face and merry black eyes, wandered up, smiling. "I'd love to make a comparison." He placed a scone on his plate and took a bite, closing his eyes in appreciation. "Lauren, your scones are good, but these are sublime." He smiled at Mia, his face crinkling into deep laugh lines, "Hello, I'm Max Davis."

"And I'm Mia Spinel. Nice to meet you." She held up her hands, laughing. "And please don't ask me for the chef's recipe. She won't give it to me either."

"That's a shame," the newcomer smiled. "I guess you'll have to keep trying out different recipes, Lauren.

36

I'll be happy to eat any rejects you have." His wiry, compact frame looked like all muscle. He could probably eat a scone basket a day and not gain an ounce.

"Yeah, don't I know it," Lauren grinned and sipped her champagne. "Why don't you have dinner with us, Mia, if you're here alone? You can give us the scoop on all the best dishes," she added conspiratorially.

"Oh, I always let Jackson, the headwaiter, tell me what to order. He always knows what's best that day." Mia added, "I'd love to join you for dinner."

"Wonderful," said Lauren, savoring her champagne. "That sounds like a great idea."

"It does, especially when you don't know what the best catch of the day is," Max agreed. "And so many Maine restaurants just push the lobster at the tourists. I like lobster, but there's a lot more to try." He made a face, wrinkles crinkling around his dark eyes, "Plus, growing up on a lobster boat takes a little of the fun out of lobster. Not that we got much of it to eat, ourselves. That was for the paying customers."

"I can imagine," Mia agreed.

Paul said jocosely, "I bet the headwaiter pushes yesterday's leftovers. That's what I'd do." His handsome face creased at his joke, and he gave a hoarse chuckle.

"Oh, I doubt that," Lauren smoothed over his comment with the ease of long practice.

A young woman joined the group, limply offering a clawlike hand with predatory red nails, "Hi,

I'm Melissa." Her extravagantly styled hair, spun to candy floss by bleach and blowdryers, cascaded down her back in elaborate waves and a strapless, fire engine red dress clung to every curve. She looked out of place in the antique-filled library, like a little girl trying too hard to be Barbie.

"Hello, I'm Mia Spinel," Mia shook her bony, limp hand.

"Ohhh, you're the hotel owner!" She gripped Paul's arm excitedly. "It's so nice to meet you!" Her voice went up shrilly at the end of each sentence. Her wide smile showed all her teeth, but never quite reached her wide open eyes, spiked with mascara.

"It's nice to meet you too, Melissa."

An older woman, encased in a bubblegum pink dress several inches too short and tight for her age and figure, joined their party. Behind her bobbled a fat man with a shiny red face, tight collar and vacant smile.

"John and Mandy, I'm so glad you're here," Lauren said. "This is Mia Spinel. Mia, these are two of my trustees."

Mia looked them over, not impressed, "How nice to meet you."

"Spinel, you must be one of the hotel owners," Mandy enthused in a syrupy sweet voice and held out her hand for Mia to shake.

"Nice to meet you, Mandy," Mia said, shaking a puffy hand full of knobbly rings and oily moisturizer. John leaned hard on a chair back for support, puffing after the short walk from the elevator.

"I absolutely love this hotel. It's so," Mandy

looked around at the grand carved fireplace and shining constellation enthroned on the ceiling, "quaint. Just marooned out here on a desert island." She smiled sweetly, smoothing her helmet of defiantly golden blonde hair. "Lauren always picks the cutest little out of the way places for company getaways."

John said, straightening up slightly, "This looks to be Mandy and my last company trip. After her birthday, this little girl's in charge of it all." He patted her arm paternally, then looked around disparagingly, "I do wish you'd chosen someplace really interesting, Lauren, like New York. All the good restaurants are there."

"Oh, Chef Ava is one of the best chefs around," Max hastily put in. "You know we don't have time for a long trip this year, John."

"And you're always welcome on any company trips, John. And Mandy too," Lauren quickly added with a soft smile. "You've done so much for me and Tisserande over the years."

Mia began having second thoughts about joining Lauren for dinner. She loved meeting new people— finding new friends was one of the joys of travel—but sometimes she got a bad feeling about an evening from the start. There didn't seem to be a smooth way to get out of it now. She liked what she'd seen of Lauren, but she just couldn't say the same for all her companions. She politely asked the newcomers, "Would you like a scone?"

"Ohhh, I couldn't possibly. Way too many carbs," Melissa said brightly, baring her teeth. "But they do look yummy!"

Mandy, patted her protruding stomach, self righteously refusing.

Lauren restarted the conversation, "What do you recommend doing around the hotel?"

Max grinned in anticipation. "I'm trying out one of the Herreshoff twelve-and-a-half's I saw at the dock. I've only admired those from afar—always wanted to sail one."

"I second that," Lauren agreed warmly. "Gorgeous little sailboats."

Mia told her, "I explored around the hotel this afternoon. I'm planning on visiting the village tomorrow. It's absolutely charming, with the most interesting artists' shops. I always find a few unique presents there."

Paul cut in, "So, Lauren, are you expecting us to work the entire time we're here?" He rolled his eyes.

"Just about," she returned with a sly grin. "Really, we have a ton of projects this summer, so I thought planning together in a new location would help us brainstorm." She looked around at her little group, smiling. "We'll meet in the mornings to strategize, have a working lunch, then play for the rest of the day. We'll meet back for one of these fabulous dinners I've heard so much about. Next week, we'll be ready to hit the ground running."

"Great, love these workaholic vacations you drag us on," Paul groused, putting his arm tightly around her shoulders, then dropping it. Lauren looked up at him, her smile fading. "Now, can I take you two lovely ladies in to dinner?" He held out his arms to Mia and Lauren.

Mia looked at his arm and laughed, smoothly bypassing it. "Oh, I don't think we need to be that formal. It is a Maine island, after all." She led the way to the main dining room, catching Jackson's eye.

The others followed, Melissa grabbing Paul's proffered arm before it dropped, giggling like a girl at prom. The rest of the Tisserande group joined their party as they headed toward the dining room, falling into line.

The imposing headwaiter promptly opened the tall doors as she approached.

Jackson murmured discreetly, "It's very good to see you again, Ms. Mia. You're joining the Tisserande party tonight?"

She nodded confirmation, and he led her to the table, already set with Mia's place. She smiled approvingly at him, and he considerately pulled out the chair giving her the best view of the room.

It was worth looking at. Originally a grand ballroom purpose-built for the critical debutante parties that married off the family's daughters, it had been transformed into a beautiful dining room. A monumental stone fireplace, orange flames dancing, stood opposite a wall of tall French doors, covered for the night by long green velvet curtains. Several carpets in varied tones from cream to blues and greens scattered across the vast acreage. Firelight flickered, filling the room with a warm glow. White tablecloths and sparkling silverware decorated every table, crowned by ornate silver candelabras rising from unique floral arrangements. Soft music played from the grand piano at the end of the room.

The flowers on Mia's table were almost a handful of wildflowers, but arranged so skillfully they enhanced the formal dining room. Several colors of hellebores, from pinks to deep burgundy, were set off by white viburnums streaked with deep purple. Every table was different and strikingly beautiful.

As she sat down, Lauren commented, "Isn't that beautiful? That's such a delightful arrangement."

"I guess red roses would clash with the curtains. Red and green, like Christmas."

Melissa looked down at her scarlet red dress, making a face. "I guess I clash with them too."

"Mel, you know you're gorgeous like always," Paul reassured her with a cheeky grin. "Red looks good on you."

Mia had planned her green dinner dress to coordinate with the dining room, as usual. She asked, "Jackson, what wonderful dishes do you have for us tonight?"

He handed menus to all, waiting patiently while they studied them. Lauren looked at hers, murmuring happily, then said, "Everything looks wonderful, but I'd love Jackson's opinion. I always defer to experts." She smiled at the headwaiter, green eyes sparkling.

Paul muttered, "Like fun you do." Melissa smirked.

Lauren ignored him, looking expectantly at the headwaiter.

42

Jackson cleared his throat. "We have a few specials today. Naturally, we have the grilled lobster, but since you are from Maine, perhaps you'd prefer a twist on that with a lobster risotto and a side of tiny fresh spring peas."

"Delicious," Lauren enthused.

"The ocean quahogs are excellent today. I highly recommend them as an appetizer with just a soupçon of lemon or as a main course with freshly made linguine."

"That's for me." Max closed his menu, handing it to Jackson.

"Is there anything without shellfish? I'm allergic," Melissa complained.

"Of course, ma'am," Jackson nodded deferentially at her. "We have a wonderful salmon, hot smoked on applewood, with new potatoes on the side."

"Can you do salad instead?" Melissa looked pompously at the rest of the table. "I'd blow up like a blimp if I ever ate potatoes."

Max smirked into his menu, trying to hide behind it unsuccessfully. Melissa glared at him.

"Of course, ma'am," Jackson told her.

"And I want just a little lemon and olive oil dressing on the side. And no spinach in the salad."

"Of course, ma'am," he repeated.

"I'm for surf and turf, myself," Paul said, closing his menu with a loud slap. "Bring on a feast." He laughed heartily. "Some beer too. Something imported."

"Yes, sir," Jackson said, his eyes narrowing ever so

slightly. Mia thought he disguised his sneer well.

Lauren said, "It's a hard choice to make, the risotto or pasta, but we're luckily here for a few days. I think I'll go with the clam linguine tonight."

Jackson nodded, looking attentively at Mia. "I'll have the risotto, Jackson. Since I'm not a Maine native, fresh lobster is always a treat for me. And I'll continue with the champagne you chose. Lovely mineral hints that will work wonderfully with seafood." Mia loved finding the perfect wine pairing for every meal. "And please bring a few appetizers to share, including one without shellfish." She nodded to Melissa and smiled at the table in general. "I want to try some of everything."

"Of course, Ms. Mia." He turned efficiently to the other side of the table, taking their orders.

Mia told Lauren, "I don't think we gave him time to finish his list of specials. I wonder what other delicious ideas he'll have for us tomorrow?"

"I can't wait to find out," Lauren said with anticipation. "You must get to dine out all the time at fabulous restaurants. That would be so much fun."

"It's one of my favorite parts of the job," Mia agreed. "I love trying different chef's dishes. Sometimes the simplest sounding ones can be the most sublime."

"Where you get the ingredients makes a huge difference," Max put in. "When I worked with my dad on the boat, the best restaurants would pay extra for us to get the better lobsters to them, fast. An hour quicker makes a huge difference in flavor."

"It does," Mia agreed. "And the individual chef makes a huge difference as well. It's like paintings, you can give the same paints to two different master artists; each will paint their own distinct masterpiece. Each chef creates their own distinctive dishes."

"Works of art," Lauren mused. "What a nice way to think about it."

"It's rather fun," Mia commented. "I try to match individual chefs with the restaurants their style works with best."

"Now that sounds like a fun job," Paul took a long swallow of beer, foam coating his upper lip. He swiped it away with the back of his hand. "Going around the world, eating at fancy restaurants. Nice life if you can get it, huh?"

Lauren said quickly, "Mia, you haven't met the rest of our little group. This is Cynthia, our vice president of finance," a painfully thin woman in a boxy orange dress and glasses to match nodded shortly. Her short, no nonsense hair was streaked in tawny brown and pale blonde, like an anemic tiger.

"Courtney Jones, one of our sales women, like Melissa," a dark, sad eyed woman with a mouth that looked like she'd just sucked a lemon said hello, nice to meet you. She didn't sound like she meant it. Rubbing her forehead like her head hurt, she sipped at her water cautiously, gripping the glass in a white knuckled hand, too delicate for her dark red nails.

"I'm Jake," one of the two men she'd seen running up the hill from the dock said, with a grandiose wave that clocked his companion.

"And I'm Blake," the other bounced back with a toothpaste ad grin, thunking Jake back with no animosity. "Two more sheets and towels salesmen."

The two men reminded Mia of large, friendly dogs, the kind that rolled in mud and you tripped over crossing the room. Well meaning, but leaving constant chaos in their wake. She wondered how they were at sales. Lauren might need a few higher end salespeople to sell her luxury lines, if this was her entire sales team.

"And this is Jeremy Tisserande Taylor, our vice president of marketing and my cousin," Lauren finished.

"Hi, you're Mia Spinel?" Jeremy pushed his glasses up his beaky nose and peered at her, squinting. "Terrific hotel you have here. I can't think why we've never been here before." He looked around the table for confirmation, and received nothing but a gentle smile from Lauren. "I mean, it's great. We should come more. And your other hotels? You've got a lot, don't you?"

"My family has a few," Mia confirmed.

"If they're anything like this, well, that's just great. It really is. Nice hotels you could bring a family to, not that I have a family. Really pretty." He subsided as his wine was poured. "Just love it." He beamed happily around the table and took a gulp of wine, wiping his mouth with a napkin.

"How long do you usually stay at a hotel?" Lauren asked curiously.

"It depends," Mia answered. "When we're setting up a new hotel or doing major renovations, I can stay

46

months. But Moose Isle is well established, so I'm just staying two weeks this trip. This is really a vacation for me."

"Got to keep the staff on their toes," Paul said boisterously. Jackson replaced his beer with a frosty glass.

Mia's smile compressed. "My manager and team here are excellent. I just like to stay familiar with all our hotels."

"That makes sense," Lauren said as her husband opened his mouth. "There's so much to do here. Sailing, hiking..."

"I can't wait to try out the spa," Melissa squealed. "It looks fab."

Mia laughed, "I always try out the spas too." She looked at Lauren, "Do you travel a lot for work?"

Lauren shook her head, smiling lopsidedly. "I'm really more of a homebody. I haven't even seen some of the factories we use—Paul's the one who takes care of that." She looked at him guzzling beer and frowned slightly. "I usually come up with new designs, do some work in distribution, help Jeremy with marketing, that sort of thing." She shrugged. "A little bit of everything."

Paul ran his fingers through his sun streaked hair, spiking it into little tufts. "Lauren's always got her fingers in every pie. Keeps us on our toes."

Max put in, "Lauren can't leave her horses for too long. More than a week and they start pining for her."

"They do," Lauren laughed good-naturedly. "I

can see them blaming me when I get back. Those big brown eyes..." She held her hand out, palm open. "I ride on the local trails in all but the worst weather. I feel so sorry for them when they're cooped up all winter." She smiled deprecatingly. "But it's really not too bad along the coast. Just a month or two when it's too icy to be safe for them most days."

"I haven't ridden a horse in years," Mia said. "That makes me want to go trail riding."

"It's the best fun there is," Lauren grinned.

Max cut in, "Next to sailing."

"Second to sailing." They grinned at each other.

"I could never ride a horse," Melissa told her. "Dirty, smelly creatures. It takes forever to get that smell off of me. And so big." She carefully placed a blonde curl over her shoulder.

Mia thought if she put that much effort into her hair, she wouldn't want to wash it often either. She gently touched her own hair, checking it was in its usual elegant place.

"I prefer cars. Fast ones," Paul took a long drink of beer. "Horses belong back in the last century."

The appetizers arrived, and conversation halted in appreciation. Jackson and the chef had selected delicately shaved smoked salmon with fresh bread, mussels with crusty French bread, and tiny spinach and goat cheese pastries. "All locally sourced, Ms. Mia."

"Perfect choices," Mia rhapsodized, and Jackson beamed with her approval.

The delicious dinner made up for the slight antagonism in the conversation. They talked of books and art, music and national parks. Paul steadily drank himself into silence, but Lauren and Max were good company. The sales team, Jake and Blake, talked exclusively to each other, with broad hand gestures illustrating their stories, which seemed largely about long past football games. Courtney, the other saleswoman, peered at the others silently from under her dark eyebrows, just pushing her food around on her plate. Mandy and John huddled together, whispering and darting little glances at the rest of the group. Mandy barely deigned to pick at her food, while John shoveled his in as quickly as possible, as if his plate would be grabbed away. Cynthia ate her meager portion quietly, watching the others from behind veiled eyes. Jeremy happily agreed with everything anyone suggested, showing no signs of original thought, but plenty of enthusiasm.

When dessert was presented, the group oohed at the towering blueberry pie slices topped with ice cream. "I know blueberry pie is such a Maine cliche," Lauren said, "but I can't get enough of it."

Paul wolfed his down. Mia saw him seriously contemplating licking the plate. He settled for loud scraping to get every crumb. Melissa had two bites, then patted her nonexistent stomach, pushing the pie away. "I can't possibly eat another bite, or I'll burst out of this dress. I'm stuffed."

Mia thought that was definitely possible, as skintight as it was.

Paul deftly dragged Melissa's plate over and started on her pie.

"I think this is the best blueberry pie I've ever had," Mia told Jackson with appreciation. "You must congratulate chef."

"Thank you, ma'am," Jackson smiled paternally. "But this dessert is not made by the hotel kitchen. There is an excellent bakery in town we have an arrangement with. The baker there is quite extraordinary."

"I'll say. Absolutely finest kind," Jeremy said, scraping his plate with happy enthusiasm. "Good birthday dinner for you, eh, Lauren?"

Lauren smiled back at him fondly. "Better than cake."

"Now," Jackson told them, "When you're finished with dinner, we have a jazz trio playing on the terrace, if you'd like to listen."

"Isn't it freezing out there?" Melissa shivered dramatically in her shiny strapless dress.

"No, no," Jackson assured them. "There's a warm fire and several heaters. It's quite pleasant."

Leaving the dining room, they went out onto the terrace. The evening sky was dark blue with tiny flashes of stars visible. Beyond the trees encircling the hotel, nothing was visible on this side of the island, just deep velvety night and the sound of the sea.

The jazz trio played at the edge of the lawn on a stage lit with large string light bulbs, giving an amber glow to the musicians. Firelight glinted off the brass saxophone and the metal of the drums. A singer with a warm chocolate voice and colorful dress sang old tunes under the stars. A square dance floor, laid out with wooden parquet, was lit with more party lights. Several couples moved together, figures glamorous in the flickering light from the massive stone fireplace.

The tables on the terrace were small and intimate, so the group spread out. Mia chose a table near the fire with Lauren and Jeremy, keeping her cashmere wrap warm around her. Slowly sipping her champagne, she enjoyed the golden bubbles dancing in the firelight.

Lauren leaned back in her chair, soaking up the atmosphere. "This is just gorgeous."

Even Jeremy was less jittery after the fabulous dinner and the bewitching ambiance. "I like this, Lauren." He looked at the lights overhead. "Do you think I could string some lights like this on my deck?" he said hopefully.

"Definitely. I'll help you put them up. That'd be a nice place for you to relax on summer evenings."

"Yeah, if only I had someone to spend them with." He looked into his champagne mournfully.

"You never know," Lauren told him. "You'll meet a lot of new people with the factory starting back up. It'll bring new people into the town. And maybe some old ones back."

"If only Deborah hadn't left," he looked fixedly at the couples dancing on the floor.

Lauren stood up, "Come on, Jeremy, I bet we can see the town lights from the other side of the island. Want to come, Mia?"

"Absolutely," Mia never turned down an opportunity to explore.

They took the smooth, well lit path around the side of the large building. It was a beautiful night, even after they'd left the champagne bubble sparkle. The smell of balsam firs hung in the air, sweet spice mixed with salty sea.

"Oh my, look at the stars," Mia breathed as they rounded the corner. The sky stretched up forever, great billows of stars forming the Milky Way. It was so vast and so beautiful, it brought tears to her eyes. She stood there a moment, blinking at the endless magnificence, then reluctantly followed the others around the building.

She could faintly see the town lights, visible in the far distance. Lauren and Jeremy walked around the corner, then she heard Lauren cry out in pain. Hurrying forward, Mia saw Lauren staring in shock at the dimly lit tableau of her husband Paul and Melissa in each others' arms. Melissa's dress was unzipped and shoved down, her bare breasts hanging. They had clearly been surprised at a very intimate moment. Their mouths hung open, miming stupefaction.

Lauren turned like an automaton, then her stunned eyes went to Mia. "May I have a hotel boat to take to town tomorrow? I'm going to need to see my lawyer immediately to start divorce proceedings." She made the statement as a stolid, unemotional expression of fact.

Mia nodded with sympathy. She wished people would keep their affairs out of her hotels. "Of course, Lauren. You can take the Harrier first thing in the morning."

52

Paul objected, "Are you serious? A divorce over this?" His pants were half off, his tie askew. He laughed scornfully, amused she would possibly take so drastic a step over his little peccadillo.

Melissa, stuffing herself back into her dress, glared at him, eyes wide behind mascara spikes. "But you said..." He cut her off with a quick hand motion.

Lauren told him, no emotion at all in her flat tone, "I appreciate you making the decision so easy for me. I should have done it a long time ago." She turned and left the two lovers, half dressed and ridiculous in the dim light.

Mia took Lauren's arm, steering her away from the unpleasant scene. Lauren walked automatically, clearly not seeing her surroundings.

Jeremy trailed behind the pair, "I say, Lauren, I say. Did you see that? I can't believe it, Paul and Melissa," he rambled in a loop.

In the light on the terrace, Mia saw how white Lauren's face was. Jeremy supported her other elbow, babbling inanities at her, but trying his clumsy best to comfort her.

Courtney and Cynthia, chatting near the fire, both stood up when they saw the little group. "What's wrong?" Courtney asked with concern. Jeremy gave them a brief explanation, then hurried to catch up.

Max following them into the hotel, worried at the look on Lauren's face, asked, "What happened? Are you okay?"

"She's fine, she's just had a shock," Mia kept her moving, away from people. "My dear, you need some space." She motioned to the concierge. "Mrs. Baker needs another room immediately. Put her near me, if possible. Mr. Baker does not need to know where she is, simply assure him she is fine."

Kayla nodded briskly and sped away.

"I can't—" Lauren started.

"But you can," Mia assured her. "You need space to process this." She looked sadly at the woman, "You didn't have any idea, did you?"

"Any idea of what?" Max demanded. "What's going on?"

Mia kept Lauren going, trusting the concierge to arrange things.

"Paul and Melissa were all over each other outside. Absolutely caught in the act," Jeremy informed him with ghoulish relish. He continued randomly patting Lauren's arm. She didn't seem to notice.

Max's face went white, then closed down. "I'll kill him." He clenched his fists.

"No," Lauren said faintly. "No, please..."

Mia spoke with authority, "Max, this isn't the time for sudden moves. Don't add complications to something Lauren's already having trouble with. Just go to bed and ask her what she wants you to do in the morning." The legal ramifications of Max attacking Paul would add to the mess and not fix anything. Why did men think with their muscles, not their brains, during stressful situations? She smiled at Lauren, "If she says beat him up, you can do it then."

Lauren smiled back in an echo of her previous

vitality, "Yes, in the morning."

"Uh huh," Max looked hard at Mia, practically dancing on the balls of his feet. "I've waited long enough. A few more hours makes no difference. You'll take care of her? I can't, for this."

"I will," Mia nodded and steered Lauren onto the elevator. Jeremy stood forlornly next to Max, wringing his hands helplessly.

Kayla met them as the elevator opened. "I've put her in room 302, directly next to you, Ms. Mia." She opened the door for them, ushering them into the room. "Shall I go get her things?"

"Yes, please, Kayla," Mia told her, settling Lauren down on the couch. "And send some hot chocolate and light the fire."

"Yes, ma'am," Kayla sped away.

Mia tucked a soft cozy blanket around Lauren, then sat down in the adjoining chair. She sighed to herself. Lauren wasn't the first friend she'd helped through her husband—or his wife's betrayal. It was a horrible thing to be betrayed by the person you trusted most.

She wasn't at all shocked Paul was having an affair with Melissa. She was a bit surprised he'd continued it at the company getaway, where his wife had a very good chance of finding out about it. Lauren was the Tisserande of Tisserande Linens, not Paul, and unless her lawyers had been very stupid, he'd be out of a job as well as the marriage if Lauren chose. Melissa certainly would be fired. Of course, philanderers were inherently untrustworthy. That was rather the point.

Kayla knocked softly and came in, bearing a tray with hot chocolate with a froth of whipped cream and a few ginger cookies, followed by a bellboy who left the luggage. "I thought she might want something to eat." She made the fire and unpacked Lauren's bags, then disappeared discretely.

Mia put the hot chocolate in Lauren's hand, "Drink a little of this." Lauren shook her head. "Just a sip or two. Sugar is good for shock—and chocolate fixes absolutely everything." Lauren sipped, and Mia took the cup back. Lauren stared at the wall in front of her, blanket wrapped tightly around her. Mia saw, with relief, her color was coming back.

Calmly gazing into the dancing flames, she was thankful she'd never had to deal with a betrayal by her husband. She'd never dreamed Leo would have an affair during his constant business trips, and he'd never had to worry about her home alone either. She'd married her best friend, and was thankful for every minute of their life together.

From her very brief acquaintance, Paul was an arrogant jerk. Lauren would probably be better off without him. But Lauren clearly loved him, at least had at some time, otherwise why would she try so hard to smooth his way through life? It was hard to know what one person saw in another. Mia stared into the fire, giving Lauren the space she needed.

After a few minutes, Lauren shook her head, "I can't believe I didn't see that one coming." She laughed harshly. "I'm an idiot."

"No, honey," Mia soothed. "You just thought

since you were trustworthy, he was too. You have to trust the person you're married to, otherwise what's the point?"

"Indeed, that's the question," Lauren's voice was rough and her eyes distant. "What's the point?"

Mia knew better than to answer that one. She'd walk away from an unpleasant lesson learned, but she'd seen too many friends go back and learn that lesson again and again. It was never a good idea to side with one member of a couple, no matter how close the friendship, and she'd just met Lauren tonight. If the couple worked out their differences, any partisan friendship was usually over.

"He's probably sleeping with her right now. In our bed," Lauren's voice rose to a high pitch.

"I doubt it," Mia reassured her. "He's probably combing the hotel to find you and apologize. He was clearly surprised when you mentioned your lawyer. I doubt he expected that," she said tartly. "I told the concierge to not say what room you're in, simply that you are fine and don't want to be disturbed." She smiled benevolently at Lauren, "I thought you'd need a little time to yourself."

Lauren smoothed the blanket around her. "You're right. I need time to decide what I'm going to do next. Besides my lawyer." She smiled crookedly and took a gulp of hot chocolate.

She said thoughtfully, "I married Paul when I graduated college. He was so handsome, so carefree. My parents died in a car crash while I was in college, and I missed them terribly. I wanted a home again. I wonder if my mom and dad would have warned me what a jerk he was? I wonder if I would have even listened?" She stared into the deep heart of the flames, gripping the soft blanket until her knuckles were white.

"I worked all the time after they died. I was either at school working or working for Tisserande. I wanted to learn as much as I possibly could. Do things right. I'd inherited the company, you know, but I don't have full control until I turn thirty, this week. I just draw a paycheck like everyone else."

She shook her head in sorrow, long dark hair falling in gentle waves around her face. "My trustees hired Paul as president after my parents died. I didn't really like the direction the company was going in, but it looked good on paper, you know? They kept telling me it was going well since profits were good. We couldn't possibly make it unless we manufactured overseas. I wasn't happy about it, but," she looked at Mia for understanding. "After all, if the company fails, no one has a job at all."

"Paul completely swept me off my feet. I completely fell for that laidback charm of his. It was so different from anything else I knew." She screwed up her face, remembering her naivety. "I hadn't really dated much. I didn't know anything. I'd dated Max, you know, way back in high school. But that fizzled when we went off to separate colleges. We always stayed good friends, but—" she spread her hands wide, "life changes things."

"A lot happens in those first few years of life on

your own," Mia added. "You learn a lot of things school didn't prepare you for."

"Well, Paul taught me about alcoholism, that's for sure." Lauren stroked the soft blanket. "He hated the idea of bringing the factories back home." She shrugged. "Makes sense, he was the one who sent most of them away." She shrugged again and pulled the blanket closer. "He's been mad about that for a long time. So I guess he starts this affair with Melissa, saleswoman of the year." Her hands clenched the blanket, crumpling it into tight folds. "I'm so far beyond mad; I don't know what to think."

"You need to take a little time, sleep on it, then think about what's next for you." Mia rooted for Lauren kicking Paul out, but she wasn't about to say that. She'd just met them this evening. It had been a very long night.

"Yes, I guess I have to decide whether to leave him or not." Lauren looked at the fire. "Or he's going to leave me and there's no decision." Her gaze turned frosty. "I doubt that, though. He'd be leaving his job and my money as well as me." She nodded once in decision. "So that leaves it up to me. Do I stay with a philandering alcoholic jerk or kick him to the curb?" She smiled crookedly at Mia. "It seems like such an obvious answer until you think of all those years together. Then it just makes me sad." She yawned, stretching her arms out like a child at bedtime.

"Sleep on it, dear," Mia soothed her. "My room is right next door, if you need anything or just want to talk." She stretched, rising to her feet. "Ring me in the morning, and we'll have a nice breakfast."

"Thanks, Mia," Lauren smiled. "I'll do that."

"Sleep tight," Mia left her alone, curled up next to the fire, with her memories of heartbreak.

4

Boat Ride

I n the morning, Mia rang Lauren's room,
receiving no answer, but when she came
downstairs, Lauren was the first person she
saw. She was striding up the hill, looking angry and
determined.

Lauren greeted her, lips tight. "I'm taking the
Harrier runabout to the mainland. I just arranged it
with the harbor master and left my bag on board.
Thanks for telling him I was coming." She flashed a
thin smile that quickly disappeared. "I'm not sure he'd
have let me borrow it otherwise."

"Are you leaving for good?" Mia wasn't sure
whether she was asking about Paul or the hotel.

"No, I want to finish the company trip. After all,
we've paid for it." She grinned crookedly at Mia, her
lips decompressing a little. "We have a few things to
plan for the next few weeks, and they've given up their
time to be here. We'll finish what we scheduled."

Lauren's smile faded. With her shoulders very erect, she said, "However, today I've made an appointment with my attorney to begin divorce proceedings. And fire Paul." She smiled grimly, lips compressed firmly. "I decided enough was enough."

"Good for you," Mia encouraged.

"Yeah," Lauren slumped a little, forced bravery disappearing. "I never thought I'd be getting a divorce." Her eyes looked forlornly at Mia, all traces of resolve disappearing.

"It's not something you go into marriage planning."

"No, it's not something I ever dreamed would happen. My parents were so happy together. I thought if I just tried hard enough, I could have that too." She squared her shoulders again and set her jaw with decision. "But that's not going to happen with Paul. I'm going to find him, and tell him what I've decided in person."

"Are you sure?" Mia wondered how Paul would react. "You did tell him you were getting a divorce last night, after all. There's no need to tell him again."

"Yes. It's the right thing to do," Lauren said, with determination.

"Good for you," Mia endorsed halfheartedly. She was a little less certain on that point. Telling Paul in person could only lead to a very unpleasant confrontation.

Lauren half smiled and put her hand on Mia's arm. "Mia," her voice choked. "Thanks, just—thanks."

"I'm always happy to help one of my friends."

She patted Lauren's hand. "I hope you'll join me for dinner again tonight."

"I'd love to," Lauren said warmly. "Now, on to battle." Shoulders thrown back and head high, she marched up the stairs.

Mia nodded and waited briefly before following her back into the hotel. She felt someone should be around Lauren when she confronted Paul. Lauren's erect figure disappeared around the corner, and Mia had a quick private word with Kayla, already back on duty.

That mission accomplished, she considered her breakfast plans.

Lauren walked reluctantly up the stairs to her husband and their shared room, planning what to say. She knew she was right to tell Paul herself, not let eight years of marriage end with that unpleasant scene last night. An ugly note to end a marriage on.

Staring at the door, her heart shrank away from the agony of divorce and betrayal. She grimaced— she'd always been a rip the bandaid off type person. This was no time to stop.

Cautiously opening the door, she ventured in. Paul stood waiting by the window. He didn't seem surprised to see her. He motioned at the window. "I saw you come up from the boats. Going to your lawyer?" He seemed only mildly curious.

Melissa sauntered out of the bathroom, leaning against the door frame like a cat marking territory. She wore nothing but a towel, suggestively slipping down her breasts. Lauren glanced at her smirk once, then away. Melissa could have him, and good riddance. This had been a long time coming. Too long.

"Yes." Lauren kept her voice calmly even. "Paul, our marriage is over. It's been over a long time. This, this incident, just made me see that clearly." She smoothed her hair back and continued, "I have an appointment with my lawyer this morning to start divorce proceedings."

He sneered, "I guess I'm fired too." He thumped the wall hard, leaving a noticeable dent in the plaster. Melissa disappeared back into the bathroom with a chipmunk squeal.

"Yes," Lauren whispered. She backed away a step, feeling for the door handle, keeping her eyes on Paul.

"After all these years," he yelled, punching the wall again. A chunk of plaster dropped to the floor. "Just taking it, doing every little thing you asked me to do." He sniggered, "Every damn thing. Can't you understand why I wanted a woman who listened to me, did what I wanted for a change?"

No joy lived in his harsh cackle. "Of course you can't, little miss perfect."

"Oh," Lauren breathed in with a gasp.

"So off you go, little miss perfect. Go live your perfect little life." He hit the wall hard, sending up a shower of plaster, and she jumped.

He hit it again, and she quickly retreated out the

door, almost bumping into the hotel employee directly outside. The man said deferentially, "Excuse me, Mrs. Baker, Ms. Mia asked me if you would be kind enough to join her for breakfast."

"Oh," Lauren began.

Paul leaned out the door. "And don't come crawling back!" He slammed the door.

Heads popped out into the hallway like meerkats, staring at her, the troublemaker. The discarded woman. Utterly humiliated, Lauren just stood there trying not to meet anyone's eyes. She saw Mandy, her trustee, shake her head in disgust and close her door, shutting her out.

The hotel employee gently took her by the elbow. "Right this way, Mrs. Baker." Expressionless, he guided her to the elevator.

She suddenly couldn't be called Baker one more time. Time to rip off the bandaid. "Call me Ms. Tisserande, please." She half smiled, "or Lauren."

The man smiled at her, brown eyes sympathetic. "Of course, Ms. Tisserande." He motioned, "Right this way."

Lauren followed him obediently, her insides still quavering from the violence of Paul slamming the door.

Mia had chosen to breakfast in a small reading room off the main library. Two cozy armchairs were tucked in next to a fireplace, perfect for reading and snoozing. Mia sat sipping coffee at a dainty table, her bright blue eyes gazing out the bay window on the far side of the room. "Oh, perfect timing," she said cheerfully. "I was just getting up the energy to order. What would you like?"

Lauren sat down, her stomach clenching like she'd been hit. "I don't know." She said flatly, "I told him."

"Good for you." Mia encouraged, "I think you're doing the right thing."

"I think," Lauren swallowed hard. She noticed her hands were shaking and tucked them next to her hips. "I think I need to eat something before I take the boat."

"Of course you do."

In just a minute, Mia placed a still warm blueberry scone in front of her. The smell was appetizing and nausea inducing at the same time. Her stomach churned. "Just take a bite," Mia urged. "You'll feel better."

Lauren took a bite, and another. The scone was very good. As it disappeared, her equilibrium returned and her hands stopped trembling.

Suddenly she remembered, "You're going to have to bill me for wall damage."

Mia looked at her questioningly.

"He hit the wall a bunch of times. It had cracks in the plaster." She shuddered and crumbled the scone onto her plate. "It was like he wanted to hit me, not the wall."

"Oh dear," Mia said, with complete composure. "Don't worry about the wall. Hotels deal with that kind of thing all the time. I'm sorry you had that happen and I'm glad you're out of it."

"Yeah, me too," Lauren's voice quavered. "I can't believe he would punch the wall like that. I could see it in his eyes. He wanted to punch me, not the wall. It's like I didn't know him at all."

Mia nodded thoughtfully. "If you'll forgive me," she cleared her throat discretely. "Sometimes people make bad decisions in a divorce. It might be best for you to stay somewhere besides your home while things are being finalized—somewhere he can't surprise you alone."

Lauren, shocked, sat there a minute, "You're right." Then she realized, "What about my home? I mean, the house was my grandparents. It has all their things. Grammy Mae's wedding china, the rocking horse my Pop built me. Do you think he'd," she shuddered, "mess with that?"

"I tell you what," Mia strategized quickly. "Do you have security at your company?"

"Yes, of course."

"Is the house yours or joint?"

"It's mine, in trust." Lauren gave a half smile. "I was meeting the lawyers after my birthday to sign the paperwork for that and the property purchase."

"You have fortunate timing for a divorce, then," Mia said, inwardly relieved. "So tell your security Paul isn't allowed on the business or your home premises without accompaniment and can't remove or damage your things. They can pack a bag for him, to start. Thankfully, you have time to arrange that since he's on the island now."

"I'll do that right now."

While Lauren was calling her security, Mia looked out the window. It looked like it might storm soon, gray, billowing clouds sat on the distant horizon.

Melissa wandered aimlessly about, graceless in stilt-like heels and abbreviated dress. Her candy floss hair was flattening in the heavy air. She constantly looked up at Paul's room like a lost puppy, visibly wondering whether he would call for her to come back. Mia saw her enhanced chest heave in decision, then she went back inside the hotel.

"Well, that's done," Lauren let out a deep breath as she hung up the phone. "My house should be safe and they're shutting down Paul's access to the company immediately." She screwed up her face. "I actually have a bunch of that sort of phone calls to make, now that I think about it. I wonder if I should see my lawyer this afternoon when they've already drawn up the paperwork."

Mia stayed silent, listening to Lauren strategize.

"I guess I'll head back to the mainland," Lauren decided. "Then listen to what they've come up with this afternoon. I'll ask Jeremy to chair meetings today." She sighed. "He tries so hard."

"Loyalty is worth a great deal," Mia commented.

"It is. I think loyalty is the most valuable quality there is." Lauren said thoughtfully, then got up. "Thanks for breakfast, Mia. I'll see you at dinner tonight?"

"I look forward to it." Mia rose, ready to start her plans for the day.

Once outside the cozy room, the peaceful calm

disintegrated rapidly. In the lobby, Melissa screeched at Kayla. Guests were giving the lobby a wide berth, while still trying to listen to the loud scene. They stood on the outskirts, avidly absorbing every word.

"What do you mean, you don't have any boats for me? I want off this island right now! You can't keep me prisoner here." Melissa strode up and down in a tight loop. Mia waited for her to snag a heel in the carpet fringe in her pointless rage.

Lauren approached Melissa, "What are you yelling about?"

"I want off this island right now," she yelled, leaning in close to Lauren's face. "This is kidnapping!"

Mia noticed Mandy, Lauren's trustee, watching the show from the elevator entrance. She smirked, clearly gloating at the embarrassing scene. When she noticed Mia looking at her, Mandy wiped her face to a syrupy concerned expression.

Kayla offered with a forced smile, "I told her the boat is scheduled to leave at two o'clock today, as usual." She checked her watch. "That's four hours from now. She can also go to the town ferry at noon. We would be more than happy to drive her to town immediately," she added desperately, clearly trying to make the scene in the lobby end.

"That's not good enough." Melissa threw out a hand, not so accidentally clawing Lauren with her talons. "You let her," she hissed at Lauren, "have a boat. I want one too."

Rubbing at the red scratches on her arm seeping blood, Lauren had had enough. She said firmly, "If a

69

boat will get her off this island immediately, give her my boat. I can go to town in the ferry, visit my lawyer, then return in the boat. You can leave the keys with the harbor master there."

"I guess that will have to do." Melissa abruptly turned on her heel. "I'll go get my bags. And tell Paul so he doesn't worry about me. He gets so protective, you know," she flung spitefully behind her.

Mia nodded meaningfully to the bellhop, and he ran after Melissa with a cart.

Lauren sighed, "Anything to get her off the island." She looked at Mia, "You don't mind, do you?"

"I wholeheartedly agree," Mia said with decision. She intensely disliked public scenes. Melissa was a magnet for them. Mia wanted her off the island immediately, by whatever means necessary.

Lauren suddenly remembered, "Oh, I left my laptop bag on the boat. I'd better run go get it." She grinned crookedly, "She'd probably throw it in the sea." She strode down the hill to the dock, energy back in her long paces.

She met Courtney standing alone on the dock and looking out at the distant fog rolling in, brown eyes forlorn as a lost puppy's. "Headed to town, Lauren?" She glanced up at her awkwardly, twisting her thin hands together, then rubbing at her forehead. "I'm so sorry about what happened. You and Paul, I mean."

"Thanks," Lauren reddened a little. "No, Melissa's taking my ride in a few minutes. Anything to get her off this island. I'll go this afternoon instead."

Lauren ran around the end of the dock and jumped on the Harrier. The bag wasn't next to the pilot's seat where she remembered leaving it. After opening a few compartments, she found it. The harbor master must have tucked it away neatly.

She returned quickly, almost running up the hill in her easy athletic stride. Giving a quick smile to Mia, "I've thought of a slew of phone calls I need to make. I want to close down joint credit cards and freeze accounts as quickly as possible. Talk to my trustees; not all are on the island. And call my lawyer again." She ran up the stairs energetically, ready to get things done.

Mia looked after her with approval. Lauren was going to be just fine. She was sensibly taking care of business, and moving forward with her life. Mia settled herself in an Adirondack chair overlooking the harbor with her little notebook and rose pink fountain pen. She needed to plan a few things herself.

In a few minutes, Melissa emerged with Paul. He kissed her long and hard, hands encircling her body, then broke off with a slap to her backside, turning to return to the hotel, before she moved a step. "Off you go, sweetheart. I'll see you back at our place," he called back loudly from the porch. He didn't bother to see her off.

Melissa gave a happy wiggle, like a puppy being praised, and left, strutting down the green lawn. The bellboy followed, grinning, cart piled high with luggage.

Mia watched her mincing walk across the lawn, clumsily tiptoeing to prevent her heels from sinking into the turf. She hoped Melissa knew how to pilot the boat. Surely, living on the Maine coast, she would have had access to a boat, wouldn't she? She didn't see Douglas or the Picnic Boat around to take her instead.

Mia drew in a calming breath of salt air, watching the bellboy load Melissa's bags into the boat. He tried to help Melissa on board. She slapped away his help, and awkwardly stumbled off her heels into the boat. The bellboy, Sam, ran to the harbor master's boathouse, grabbing the key and a puffy orange life vest.

He handed the life vest to Melissa, who stepped back, clearly objecting. Sam gestured for her to wear it, and she finally agreed. Mia grinned at the teenager ineptly trying to strap the puffy vest around Melissa's inflated chest. With a gesture toward the mainland, he obviously offered to pilot her to the town dock. She responded with a petulant shake of her head. Reluctantly, he handed her the key, and stepped off the boat.

Melissa started the engine, and Sam hurriedly untied the dock lines as the boat strained against the dock. The engine roared as the boat was freed, and after a slight false turn, Melissa steered the boat away from the island. Mia grimaced slightly, eyes tracking her uncertain progress. The boat swung in a large uncoordinated arc, heading for Southwest Harbor.

The roar of the engine broke with a sharp cough and the boat sheered off plane. With a sudden whoosh, flames roared high and the air rattled.

Debris scattered all around where the boat and

Melissa had been, just a minute ago, but there was no boat—and no Melissa. The disturbed water swirled, quickly swallowing all traces of the boat. Mia ran down to the dock, followed by Sam, looking very young and scared. Freckles blotched his white face. She couldn't see Melissa's bright orange vest anywhere in the water, as hard as she strained to see.

Joseph's long legs flew down the hill, grabbed a key and life jackets from the boathouse, and roared off in one of the staff boats with Sam bundled aboard. Mia had never seen him move that fast before. She stood on the dock, eyes straining for a glimpse of a bright orange life vest.

The sound of the explosion drew guests and employees outside. The crowd huddled at the edge of the dock, trying to see what Joseph was doing—would he find her in the churning water? Whispers spread through the crowd like wildfire.

Sam piloted the boat in slow sweeps around where Melissa's boat had disappeared, while Joseph fished the flotsam with a long boat hook. There wasn't much left in the water.

Max and Jeremy ran to Mia, faces white in horror.

"Lauren?" Max couldn't finish the question.

Jeremy stood, mouth gulping for air, unable to talk. His eyes desperately scanned the ocean.

Mia shook her head quickly in reassurance. "Lauren's fine, in the hotel. Melissa was alone on the boat."

They both breathed a sigh of relief. "Thank God,"

Max said thankfully, bowing his head briefly. He looked at the scene, fragments of boat scattered on the gray ocean. He suddenly heard what he'd just said.

"I know, it's the wrong thing to say. There's no way Melissa survived that. What an awful way to go." He stared out at the gray water. "No way she survived that," he repeated dully.

"Terrible." Mia could see a police boat and several other boats coming from the harbor to help in the pointless search. She shivered in the wind, suddenly cold to her bones. No sign of a bright orange life vest in that gray eddying water.

"I don't think they're going to find her," Jeremy said aloud what they were all thinking. He looked at the boats milling around the site desultorily.

"No, let's go back inside where it's warm," Mia agreed, bowing her head at the tragedy. "There's no point in standing here." The day had turned overcast, heavy fog rolling in from the ocean. The air felt thick, almost difficult to move through.

The crowd turned their backs on the blank slate of the sea and began a slow funeral procession up the lawn, sending quick glances back at the boats searching for Melissa.

At the top of the hill, they met Cynthia staring at the searching boats. Her face was white and her breath came in short, sharp pants. Her streaked hair stood up in spikes, as if she'd been pulling hard at it. "Was that Lauren? Have they found her yet?"

"No," Max told her heavily. "Melissa."

"Melissa..." She swallowed hard, mind furiously

working. She looked at him, eyes magnified by the orange framed glasses. "She's dead? Melissa? She couldn't have survived that, surely?"

"I'd guess." Max nodded noncommittally and went inside.

Lauren slowly walked down the main steps, looking with confusion at the people running around the lobby. Max ran straight to her, arms wrapping around her in a bear hug, reluctantly releasing her after a brief embrace. Jeremy called out, "Lauren, thank God!" and ran to her, hugging her, then awkwardly patting her on the arm.

"What happened? I heard a loud noise..."

"We thought we'd lost you for a minute." Jeremy still looked shaken. He gave her one last hug, as if making sure she was really there, then backed off, grinning foolishly at her. "Glad you're still here, cousin," he said fervently.

"Me too," Lauren looked confused. "But what happened? The noise? It sounded like an explosion?"

Max took hold of both of her upper arms. "Lauren, honey, listen. Melissa's probably dead."

"More than probably," Jeremy added helpfully. "No way she survived that."

Max repeated, "More than probably." He gripped her arms tightly. "The boat exploded. The boat you were going to take, exploded."

Lauren looked out at the searching boats. "Exploded?"

Mia clarified, "The boat exploded—flames everywhere. I doubt there is much left of," she paused, "anything."

Lauren sagged, even with Max holding her up. He steered her to a chair where she collapsed, her knees clearly unable to hold her up. "Oh, no."

"I'm afraid so," Mia looked out at the rescue attempt. "I don't think they're going to find her."

"No, I don't see how they could." Max looked out at the undulating wave of white coming across the water. "There's a fog mull rolling in. No way they'll see anything in that." He shook his head dully. "Doubt there's anything to see. Hardly anything left on the water after that."

The boats seemed to agree with him, slowly widening their search, some aimlessly heading back to the harbor, zigzagging as they went, as if to say they hadn't really given up hope yet.

Paul strode across the lobby, shoving past shaken guests, then stopped at their huddled group. "What are you looking so upset for?" he yelled at Lauren. "Aren't you glad she's dead? That's what you wanted, isn't it?"

Lauren spread her hands out in supplication. "No, no, of course not." Her voice wobbled with uncertainty.

"So how did you kill her?" he threw at her.

"The boat just exploded, huh? You put a bomb in it? What'd you do?" He took a menacing step toward her. "What'd you do?"

Lauren said faintly, shrinking into herself, "Of course not."

"Is that an accusation?" an official voice inquired, cutting like ice. The police officer had entered the room unobtrusively. His commanding voice radiated control.

"It sure is," Paul condemned, turning to the police officer. "I'll say she did it."

"And your name is?" The officer wrote in his black notebook, his stubby fingers printing neatly. "Very well, I'll call you for an interview shortly."

The policeman turned his attention to Lauren. "And your name is?"

"Lauren Tisserande," she forced it out, "Baker."

Paul jeered at her discomfiture, face twisted mockingly.

"Tisserande, eh? Like the factory that fired everyone?" She saw his face change to anger. "And you and this gentleman are?"

"My soon to be ex-wife," Paul cut in. "My soon to be wife just died in that explosion." He pointed an accusing finger at Lauren. "And she killed her." His twisted face reddened with each word.

"I see." The policeman wrote firmly in his notebook. "I would like to request that you two," and he gestured at the huddled group, "and any of you connected with Ms. Melissa Hathway, please stay on the island, and make yourselves available for questioning." He snapped his notebook shut like a mousetrap. "Investigations on the cause of the explosion are proceeding." He nodded, looking at the little group suspiciously. "Sorry for your loss." He left as unobtrusively as he'd appeared.

5

Questioning

Lauren took a deep breath, shuddering as she exhaled. "Okay, so we need to plan."

"You need a lawyer, right now," Jeremy told her, pushing his glasses up his nose. He looked after Paul, the angles on his face standing out sharply.

"Yes," she agreed. "I'll tell Uncle Harvey to come here instead." She texted briefly. While she waited for the reply, she told them, "We have the conference room booked for the day. Let's meet there so we can tell everyone who doesn't know what happened." She smoothed her long dark hair, repositioning the clip holding it back. "I don't know anyone who could have missed hearing the explosion, but we should meet as a company."

She shook her head sadly, "Poor Melissa. What an awful way to go."

Her phone beeped and she looked down. "Okay, my lawyer is taking the regular ferry into town." She looked at Mia, "Can someone from the hotel meet him in town? Uncle Harvey's not much of a walker."

Mia motioned to Kayla and the concierge hurried over, brimming with helpful curiosity.

"I'll send a golf cart to meet the next ferry," Kayla told Lauren. "Is there anything else I can do?"

"Can you make an announcement or something?" Lauren asked. "I want my company to meet in the conference room."

Mia explained to Lauren, "We only do fire alarm emergency announcements over the speakers, but Kayla will know where everyone in your group is and round them up for you. In about half an hour?"

Kayla nodded agreement, eager to help.

"Perfect." Lauren slumped a little, then straightened up. "Well, that's our game plan. Shall we three go ahead to the meeting room?"

"I'll send snacks and coffee," Kayla offered.

"Thanks." She waved goodbye to Mia and slowly headed down the hall between Max and Jeremy, clearly planning hard.

Kayla paused a minute before running to her tasks, "Wow, just wow."

"Agreed," Mia looked out the window at the white fog haze. She couldn't even see the hotel dock now.

"Do you think it was an accident?" Kayla asked, nodding out the window.

"I don't see how it could have been," Mia said slowly. "Boats don't just blow up, in my experience. And Douglas treats them all like his children. They're meticulously maintained, to say the least."

Kayla asked curiously, "Do you think Ms. Tisserande killed that woman?"

Mia looked at Kayla. "Does she seem the type to you?" she asked, wondering about the concierge's opinion. Concierges always knew everything about their guests. It was their job to read people quickly.

Kayla looked after the little group thoughtfully. "No, she really doesn't." She told Mia, "I would have kicked that husband of hers to the curb and cheered my freedom. Plus, she's got that handsome guy next to her to fall back on. And she owns the company, not him. Why would she kill anyone?" She shrugged a little. "Maybe it was a terrible accident, after all?"

"I hope somehow it wasn't murder. Hopefully, that's what the police will decide. I'm not sure how they could ever know for sure with the boat at the bottom of the sea, however." She looked out into the all encompassing fog and shuddered. "Of course, then the hotel will probably be responsible for Melissa's death." Mia shook herself into action. "All right, Kayla, please get those errands started. Then I want extra team members in the library and lobby to answer the guests' questions. I don't want a line of guests asking questions. I know we don't have a lot of answers yet, but we'll tell the guests when we do. Just having hospitality team around to answer quickly what they do know makes a difference. Also, put out lots of nibbles and hot cider, not coffee. We don't need extra caffeine. Cookies and a hot drink always calm things."

"Right away, Ms. Mia," the tiny blonde dynamo sped off, spiky hair standing straight up.

Mia smiled and went to her room to make her own phone calls. Her children were not going to be pleased with her news.

Lauren looked at her remaining company management and sales team sitting around the big conference table. No one met her eyes except Max, smiling encouragingly.

She stood there a minute, uncertain what to say. Then she put her hands on the table, leaning toward the group. "Well, this weekend isn't what we expected from our big company retreat, is it?" She smiled crookedly. "I think next time we'll just go on a picnic."

Jake and Blake stifled guffaws of laughter, snorting. Courtney sat stiffly beside them, mouth prim and pain filled brown eyes looking only at the table.

Lauren gave Jake and Blake a look. They stilled instantly. "I guess you all know by now Melissa and Paul were," she swallowed hard, "having an affair." She paused a heartbeat, forcing herself to continue. "I don't know who here already knew about it, but I only found out last night." Face crimson in embarrassment, she added, "I fired Paul this morning. I was headed to my lawyer's today to start the divorce process this afternoon."

"Good riddance," Max cut in, meeting her eyes.

Jake added, "Paul is totally immature."

"Totally," Blake added, feet propped comfortably

on the table.

"Melissa took the boat I'd borrowed. She wanted to get off the island as quickly as possibly after—" she hesitated, forcing her voice not to shake, "she took the boat instead of me." She held up her hands. "The boat blew up with her on it." Her voice failed her.

Cynthia said, "Such a terrible tragedy."

Lauren's hands clenched on the table, then she nodded. "This tragedy takes first priority now."

"Some loss," Courtney said with venom, just under her breath. Her face briefly twisted in hate. Lauren gave her a quick glance, curious at her vindictive hatred of a dead woman.

She spoke louder, straightening her spine. "Melissa was not," she paused, "my favorite person at the moment."

"I'll say," Jake called out, smirking. Blake leaned back in his chair, rocking slowly.

Lauren continued, "but she worked with us for a year and her death is a tragedy." She nodded sharply. "So let's have a moment of silence, of respect for Melissa's life and this terrible tragedy."

They all bowed their heads and closed their eyes, reverting to their childhoods, praying in church. Feet moved surreptitiously on the floor, settling into a comfortable position, a muffled cough, the ticking of the antique clock on the mantle echoing loud in the silence. Lauren counted the tick tocks. One, two, three —when she reached sixty, the deafening silence had nearly overwhelmed her. She opened her eyes and cleared her throat harshly. That had been hell, but it was the right thing to do.

Max banished the silence. "So what are your plans now, Lauren?"

The door banged open. Mandy burst in the room, trailed by John, shuffling his feet along.

"Laurie, sweetie pie, are you okay?" She encased Lauren in well padded, bubblegum pink arms, trapping her neatly. "When I heard the news I knew I had to find you immediately." She finally released Lauren. "Why ever did you kill Melissa?" Her bloodshot eyes looked deeply into Lauren's, feigning concern. "I mean, I didn't like her either, but why not just fire her?"

Blake's feet thunked to the ground as he had a coughing fit.

"Excuse me?" Lauren asked, completely confused.

Mandy kept hold of Lauren and continued, cloyingly sweet, "I know you were jealous of the attention Paul was paying to Melissa, but really, sweetie, why kill her? It wasn't like he would really have an affair with gutter trash like her. He was just being nice." She continued, her marshmallow arms firmly encircling Lauren's waist, "I'm sure him telling you to leave this morning would," she gestured, dirty rings hampering her movement, "just have blown over. He would have taken you back, forgiven you."

"Excuse me?" This time Lauren's voice was icy. She extricated herself from the smothering embrace and stepped away from her trustee. "What exactly do you mean by that?"

"Now, Mandy, I'm sure it was just a terrible accident." John patted Lauren's arm with a fleshy hand,

84

florid red cheeks rounded in an insincere smile. "The boat's on the bottom of the ocean. No one can prove a thing. Not a thing," he reassured her inanely. His piggy eyes shifted, clearly wishing he was somewhere else.

"But, John, how is Lauren going to get the help she so desperately needs, if she won't admit what she's done?" She bared her teeth in a smile at Lauren. Her close-set eyes, ringed with stiff black spikes of brittle lashes, stayed wide and gloating. "She has to confess."

Lauren finally took control. "Mandy, I have no idea what you're talking about." She spoke firmly, with her back military straight.

"But, sweetie pie, I just want you to get help. I know this shrink who can help you. You go there for a few years and when you get out, it'd be like nothing happened. Paul can take care of the company while you're gone. We'll take care of everything. You don't need to worry about a thing." She put her hands on her ample hips, laying down the law with honeyed tones. "We're your trustees. You have to do what we say." She oozed an insincere smile, "We just want you to get the help you need."

Lauren broke in, shaking her head, "Mandy and John, you're being ridiculous. One of my employees just died tragically. We have no idea yet what happened exactly, but I certainly had no part in her death."

"Of course, it's not really your fault," John suggested, backing away warily.

"I think you both need to leave this meeting now," Lauren said firmly.

"Shouldn't Paul be here? In a company meeting?" Mandy's bloodshot eyes searched hopefully for Paul. "You can't hold a company meeting without your CEO."

"Paul's not here," Lauren stated flatly. "If you would both leave, we need to continue this meeting."

"Well, I never..." Mandy was speechless, hands on her hips in resentment. John lumbered out the door, with her reluctantly following him, clacking her heels petulantly on the wood floor.

Lauren smoothed her hair and cleared her throat again. "Well, that was—different." She struggled for words, cheeks flaming in embarrassment.

Jake unexpectedly came to her defense, "Hey, no one here thinks you killed Melissa. That's crazy. Why would you?" He nodded shortly and started doodling boats on his paper again.

Blake added, "Not that someone didn't kill her. Boats don't just blow up. But you absolutely wouldn't do that. I mean, why would you?" He repeated, eyes darting around the room. He puffed out his cheeks, then let it out explosively. "That woman is something else."

"She's nuts," Jake backed Blake up.

Lauren forced a laugh. "She certainly is." She took a deep breath, calming herself. "It's probably a good thing their trusteeship of the company ends this week." She tapped her pen on the paper, collecting her equilibrium, and trying to remember what she'd planned to accomplish at this meeting, besides total humiliation. "Our company plans are almost exactly what they were before. Obviously without Melissa—and Paul."

"Doesn't he get a say in the company? He's your husband still and he was CEO before he married you." Cynthia pushed her bright glasses up her nose, peering at Lauren. "Mandy is a little—I'll not say anything bad about her," she pursed her lips, "but Paul is CEO."

"Not any more. I fired him this morning. He's no longer involved with Tisserande. The company is still held by my trust and my trustees," she glared out the door, "until my birthday this week," Lauren stated. "I suppose he might collect salary for an extra day or two if they insist, but that's it." She looked at her list of tasks, then decided to explain further.

"Harvey Thompson, my lawyer, is on his way here to discuss," she cleared her throat, "my future plans. But we're going forward with the land acquisition and new factory, as before. Nothing has changed on that front. I own the company, and the trust is broken when I turn thirty. And I want that factory built and operational in our town as soon as possible."

"So," she looked at her sales team of three, "We're going to have a lot of sheets to sell." She grimaced, "Look, I know Melissa was the top saleswoman this year, but I need you to plan your strategies without her. I know it's a lot to ask, so soon after this—" her voice cracked, but she managed to continue, "—this tragedy." She shook her head, trying to shake off shock, "But we'll still need to make this work."

Jake and Blake started laughing, then abruptly stopped, clearly remembering Melissa was now dead.

Courtney said bitterly, "Melissa couldn't sell anything, especially not high end linens. The only reason she was top saleswoman was..." She broke off and rubbed her temple with delicate red tipped fingers, deep brown eyes narrowed in resentment of the dead woman.

Blake sniggered, leaning back in his chair. Jake stifled a braying laugh and doodled more boats.

Lauren finished, "She was sleeping with Paul and that made her top saleswoman." She looked around the room. "Apparently, there's a lot going on I don't know yet."

Courtney summed up caustically, "Let's just say you don't have an immediate need for another salesperson." Her knuckles whitened on her pen. "Melissa's sales weren't much to brag about."

"I see." Lauren straightened her spine again, feeling tight muscles stretching across her back. "How's the new higher end line going? You have the samples Max gave you?"

Courtney replied cautiously, "Paul said to slow track that, focus on the cheap stuff, it made more profit." She shrugged, "He gave us smaller commissions if we sold the higher end stuff so..." She held out her fine boned hands, "He was the boss."

"I see." Lauren said evenly, inwardly furious. "Well, as I am now the boss, I want to turn our main interests to higher quality products. We can't compete much longer by driving down prices and lowering quality. That strategy is just a race to the bottom. We'll be in serious trouble if we keep on that track. Tisserande's future is in high quality linens at a fair price."

Jake piped, "Yes, ma'am, whatever you say."

"You're the boss," Blake banged his chair legs to the floor. "I'll sell whatever you say to sell."

Jake added in sorrow, "I'll have to buy a tie if I'm selling to fancy places." He caressed his neck, clearly imagining a silk noose tightening around it.

Cynthia added with careful precision, "I think you might be right, Lauren." She paused, planning her next statement carefully. "As the Finance VP, I've been extremely concerned about us overextending to meet big box store price demands. There are several products we seem to actually lose money on in order to sell them at what that market will bear." She sat back in her chair, crossing her legs.

"Really?" Lauren said, aghast. "I didn't realize that." Her hands clenched on her notebook.

Cynthia gave a tight smile. "No, I don't imagine you did, with how I was instructed to structure my reports. By Paul, of course." She went on, lips pursed tightly in thought. "I think, if Paul is no longer involved, we need to have a serious discussion about several of Tisserande's product lines. Even cheap fabric has been going up in price dramatically, and that drastically affected our profit margin."

"Right," Lauren said with decision. "I clearly have been missing a lot."

"You weren't told a lot," Cynthia stated bluntly.

Her eyes half hid under her tawny bangs.

"Can we still build the Megeso Point factory?" Lauren asked, clearly terrified of the answer. Her hand stroked her smooth dark hair, resettling its clip.

Cynthia considered a long minute, tapping her pen on the table with sharp metallic clicks. "The final numbers you have should be accurate, as far as they go. I don't know about the company's capital. Paul handled those funds. I simply manage the day to day income and expenses and write up the reports I'm told to write." Her bony hand continued to tap the pen thoughtfully, pursing her tangerine painted lips, then she said, "There should be ample funds to build the Megeso Point factory. However, I don't know how luxury sales will do. That's not my department, I simply report on what happens. Some of the other business, especially the lower end lines, you might need to reevaluate in our current economic climate. Overseas factories aren't necessarily the cost saving advantage they were."

"Okay. That's a lot to take in." Lauren gulped coffee. "Well, the police are investigating Melissa's death, of course. I'm not sure if they know she was murdered or it was a terrible accident yet, but they want everyone connected with Melissa to remain on the island for now."

"You mean we can't leave the island?" Cynthia's pen tapped quick staccato notes. Her whitened knuckles clutched the pen, veins bulging with strain.

Max soothed, "I'm sure it won't be for long." He was leaned back, relaxed in his chair, drinking the excellent coffee with appreciation. "Not like it's a bad place to be stuck."

"I guess we were planning to be here anyway," Cynthia said grudgingly. She recrossed her thin legs. "We might as well make the best of it."

"Exactly." Max put his coffee on the table. "We planned to work and play, so we'll get some work done. Possibly not as much as we'd planned, but we will do everything that can get done now. And maybe we won't play as much as we planned, under the circumstances, but I'm sure we'll get something fun in. It's a nice place." His reassuring eyes sought Lauren's.

"Wait a minute," Courtney squeaked. "You mean the police are really investigating Melissa's death? Mandy wasn't just on one of her crazy rants?" She nervously wrung her hands. "Why would the police investigate a boat accident?"

Blake laughed snidely. "Boats don't just blow up, sweetheart."

Jake added with ghoulish relish, "She was so murdered."

Lauren said soberly, "I don't think you have much to worry about, Courtney. I was taking the boat to town this morning to see my lawyer. I told Melissa she could use it when she wanted to leave the island in a hurry. I even grabbed my laptop off the boat right before she left on it." She flattened her hands out on the table, looking down at their square cut, plainly varnished nails. "I think I'll probably be their chief suspect. My trustees certainly seemed to think I am." She laughed bitterly, "What the police don't realize is after the initial shock of his affair, I was just relieved to get rid of Paul. Melissa might not have been my favorite person today, but I certainly didn't kill her. I just fired her."

"Of course not," Jeremy said fervently. "You'd never do something like that." He tapped his fingers on the table. "Maybe it was just an accident. I wonder if they can dredge up the boat to investigate."

"Channel's wicked deep there," Max commented. "And with the current, there's a long sweep of coast it might be in."

Lauren choked a little, "I hope they can find out what really happened to Melissa. Examining the boat would be a good way to find out. And," she gulped hard, "I wish they could find her body for burial."

"Let's hope they can." Max's dark eyes were worried, despite his relaxed posture.

"So, Uncle Harvey's on his way, representing the company and me, and we all need to be available for police questioning. If anyone else feels like they need a lawyer for questioning, tell him and he'll set it up. The police chief doesn't seem the—" she paused and regrouped. "He really hates Tisserande because of the layoffs. Mostly me, but I don't want that antipathy spilling over to my employees." Lauren looked around the room. "It sounds like I might not be the only one who preferred Melissa out of the picture, even if none of us actually wanted her dead. I don't intend to let them—or my trustees—put me in jail for something I didn't do. I also don't want any of you harassed for something you're innocent of. So if you feel like you

92

need a lawyer, we'll get you one for your interview." Her nod was sharp and final. "Now, let's get to the business we're here to do."

She straightened up, all business. "Cynthia, I need to know exactly what products we have that are profitable and which we need to trim. Can you give me good breakdowns of all of our products by this afternoon? Let me see what you think I need to know first, then I'll tell you what else I want." Cynthia nodded, her scrawny hands taking quick notes in spiky handwriting.

Lauren assessed her sales team. "Okay, Courtney, you're in charge of the new made in USA luxury line. Let me see your game plan by tomorrow morning. That okay with you, Jeremy?" she asked her Marketing VP.

"Ayuh," Jeremy agreed.

Jake and Blake shuffled their feet as she turned her gaze on them. "Nothing for you two until after I see Cynthia's numbers and know what lines we're focusing on and what we're dropping. Then I'll want a detailed sales plan from you." She nodded at Jeremy, "You'll want to be in on the marketing for those."

"Whatever you say, cousin. I'll draft a statement for the press about Melissa's death right away. We need to get in ahead of the rumors." His forehead furrowed as he pushed up his sliding glasses. "I'm concerned about Cynthia's sales figures too. I wonder if we've been marketing the right stuff? Or to the right people?" He scribbled notes on his laptop, tapping rapidly.

Max grinned at Jake and Blake, "Lucky dogs, you just got the day off." He looked up at Lauren, "What do you want from me?"

She smiled crookedly at him. "You know what you need to do to organize the factory build better than I do."

He grinned back, "Yeah, I do."

Chief White began his interview with Mia and Joseph Curry in the manager's office. The chief brooded behind Joseph's antique mahogany desk, disposable pen and black notebook precisely aligned on the smooth dark wood. Fingers steepled aggressively, he looked ready to repudiate every word they said.

Joseph began his story, his pants still damp and shirt askew from his fruitless rescue attempt. "I was standing on the front porch looking at the weather. I have a group scheduled for the town lobster boat tour later today, but the fog looked like it was rolling in. I didn't want my guests to go all the way to town to find out the tour had been cancelled." He crossed his legs uncomfortably, creasing the wet wool. His British accent seemed to grate on Chief White.

"Yes?" the chief barked impatiently.

"I saw Paul Baker and Melissa Hathway come out together. Sam, the bellhop, had her luggage in his cart." He explained, "Kayla had told me Ms. Melissa Hathway had made a scene in the lobby and been offered use of the boat in order to leave immediately." He glanced at Mia and she nodded agreement. "That was unusual. We don't normally lend boats to departing guests. However, we also dislike public scenes disrupting the hotel and the remainder of her party was remaining on the island," he continued in a prim tone. "Paul Baker went inside. I stayed, watching the fog and Ms. Hathway."

"Any reason?" Another bark. The paper remained blank, steepled fingers blocking their words.

"As I just explained, we don't normally lend boats in that manner. Sam put her in the life vest. She refused his help with the boat. Douglas had readied the boat for Mrs. Baker, earlier that morning, so there wasn't anything else for Sam to do. From here, it looked like Sam offered to simply run her over to the town dock, but you'll have to ask him that." He shivered sharply, stiff, damp clothes scratching against the leather chair. "I'm glad he didn't."

Chief White hunched over his notebook, grunted, almost baring his teeth at them.

Joseph coughed and continued his story, "Ms. Hathway swung out in a large arc and seemed under reasonable control, then she turned back toward the town. The boat exploded without any warning." He recrossed his legs, awkward for once. "I ran to see if I could rescue her." He shivered again, smoothing his rumpled hair. "The biggest piece we found was an orange scrap of the life vest. She completely disappeared."

"You're sure she was on the boat when it exploded? She couldn't have jumped overboard?"

"No chance of that. I saw her standing at the console when it turned." He shifted in his chair.

The chief wrote that down, dark brow furrowed. "Odd they found nothing of the body, then."

"It was quite an explosion," Mia said in explanation. "I was sitting and watching the boat." She nodded at Joseph. "I also was a little concerned about Melissa's ability to pilot the boat. She didn't look overly comfortable around boats. I never dreamed of anything like this happening."

"No..." the chief growled thoughtfully.

"Do you know what caused it to blow up?"

"My investigations are proceeding," he stated frigidly. "May I ask you for any other information you have about Ms. Melissa Hathway?" He looked demandingly at Mia. "I understand you had dinner with her last night?"

"With the Tisserande company group, yes," Mia confirmed.

"So you're buddies with Mrs. Baker, eh?" he accused.

"I only met Mrs. Baker last night," Mia explained. "She seems nice, but I don't know her."

"You still liked her enough to have dinner with her?"

"I often have dinner with my guests," Mia explained. "I enjoy getting to know people."

"Huh," he grunted. "This morning, after her

death, Mr. Paul Baker stated he was going to marry Ms. Hathway. Is that correct?" he snapped, forcing her into a statement.

Mia inwardly sighed, stating the facts as undramatically as possible. "Last night, Mrs. Lauren Baker surprised Mr. Paul Baker and Ms. Hathway in an extremely compromising situation." She coughed delicately. "I was present. Mrs. Baker immediately requested the boat in the morning to see her lawyer about a divorce."

"I see. Mrs. Baker decided on the basis of that one incident to obtain a divorce from her husband of many years." The chief wrote in his notebook, words spilling down a dark angry line. Mia tried unobtrusively to read what he wrote but the chief guarded it too closely. "So Mrs. Baker was scheduled to take the boat, but Ms. Hathway did instead?"

"Yes."

"Her husband, Paul Baker, saw the deceased off." He aligned his pen precisely on the paper. "Anything else you can tell me?"

"Not that I can think of," Mia stated. Joseph nodded agreement.

"Then if you'll send in Mrs. Baker for questioning next." He nodded once in sharp dismissal.

Mia volunteered, "I believe, after Mr. Baker's public accusation, she called her lawyer, and he's on the way."

"I see. Already got her lawyer lined up, eh." He attacked his notebook, then carefully realigned the black pen. "Then it would be more productive for me to see Mr. Paul Baker next, if I don't have to wait for his lawyer. Please send him in." He nodded again in a firm dismissal, looking down at his nearly blank notepad. Mia feared what was going through his mind.

After they closed the door, Joseph said, "I wouldn't like to be Lauren Baker right now."

"No, she's in a difficult place," Mia agreed. "I believe I'll find out a bit more about what's going on."

"Since he's taken over my office, I had better find somewhere else to work. And some dry clothes." He sneezed, then smiled at her. "Do you have any suggestions for improving morale among the guests?"

"Just the usual of employees answering questions, drinks and nibbles," Mia told him. "And reassurance that boats don't usually explode. At the moment, it can't be much fun for them being on an island with no other way off but by boat," she laughed at the unfunny situation. "However, it's not as if the wedding party is going to cancel on us since they're already here, so we just make sure their event is a rousing success. Unfortunately, we don't have a lot of information to give the guests yet."

"No," Joseph said smoothly, "but I will think of something." He ambled off to keep the hotel running smoothly.

Mia went down to the dock, noticing the little clumps of gossiping guests staring out at the channel. She wanted to talk with Douglas before he left again to ferry people back to town. She found him in the Picnic Boat with the engine compartment wide open. He responded to her greeting with an impatient grunt, sitting up and wiping his sweaty face with a red bandanna.

Mia didn't waste small talk on Douglas. He didn't appreciate his valuable time being frittered away. "Why did that boat explode?" she demanded.

"Dunno." Douglas heaved himself out of the opening, standing up with a back cracking stretch and tucking the bandanna in his pocket. "Nothing wrong with this one, at least. Of course it's locked up a bit more than the Harrier—harder to mess with. I don't want any surprises on the afternoon boat ferry."

"Could Melissa have done something wrong and caused the boat to explode?"

"Nah, she was as numb as they come, but even she could get the boat to the harbor over there. Worst that would happen in that weather is someone would need to tow her a ways. Wasn't nothing she did to make it explode."

"Then what happened?" Mia said in frustration.

"Coulda been the bilge blower stopping. Fumes build up," Douglas considered, wiping his sweaty face. "Coulda been a spark plug loosened and gas splashed around it. Time bomb, that." He looked at her, silver blue eyes shrewd in his tanned weatherbeaten face. "Depends on if someone wanted her dead."

"It does," Mia agreed.

"Could be the other woman, the one who was going to take the boat first." He spat thoughtfully off the dock.

"That someone wanted dead or that set a time bomb?" Mia asked.

"Ayuh," Douglas replied noncommittally. "I got it ready for her like you told me, then did my morning town trip, as usual."

"Would Lauren have time to do any of those things if she just ran to the boat and back?"

"Maybe," Douglas considered, silver bright eyes looking across the water. "If she knew what she was doing wouldn't take but a minute. I wasn't watching close." He wiped his forehead. "She seemed to know boats pretty well when she came on the island. Liked this one," he patted the gleaming wood of the Picnic Boat fondly. "Grew up on the coast, she said." He looked out where his Harrier had sunk. "The other one didn't know nothing about boats." He shook his head mournfully. "What a way to go."

Mia wondered whether he meant the boat or Melissa. She looked out at the water where the boat had sank and shivered.

"Of course, the one supposed to be on it was the rich one, right? So maybe more people wanted her dead. Liked her better than the other. It would be a quick job to rig it either way." He shook his head thoughtfully. "Hard tellin' not knowin'." He shrugged and lovingly polished shining brass with a cloth, clearly ready for her to leave him alone with his lady.

"I'll leave you to it, then."

Douglas returned to his boat inspection, and Mia strolled thoughtfully up the hill. The grand white hotel was shadowed in darkness, overhung by big gray storm clouds.

The first person she saw when she returned to

the porch was Jeremy, off on one side, rocking frantically. His mournful brown eyes looked off at the distant water.

"Hi, Jeremy," Mia said quietly, trying not to startle him.

He jumped anyway, racketing the rocker runners on the wood porch. "Oh, hi, Mia. Wow, it seems like a million years since this morning." He pushed his glasses up his nose, veiling his eyes behind the heavy frames, but still looking out at the endless bleak ocean.

"It does," Mia took a nearby seat, rocking gently. "I'm so sorry about Melissa Hathway's death."

"Yeah, me too." Jeremy's rocking speed increased. "I mean, after last night, I'd have fired her, even if Lauren didn't. I mean, it was obvious she was going to be fired by someone." He shook his head, rocking like a frantic squirrel. "But I didn't want her dead, just out of the company. She wasn't really a bad person, just not great at sales. Just a kid, really." He looked out to sea, rocking spasmodically. The uneven rhythm made Mia's jaw tighten.

"I'd wanted to fire her for months because of poor performance, but Paul always insisted she was the best saleswoman in the department, and Cynthia always backed him up." He took off his glasses and wiped them sadly on a cloth, then covered his eyes again. "Not a week went by that one of the others wouldn't come complaining to me about how Paul handed her a deal they'd worked their butts off on. No way she could have pulled all those sales off. Courtney hated her guts, poor girl. Melissa stole sale after sale from her." He looked at Mia. His glasses had slipped down his sharp nose again. "I think Courtney was getting ready to leave us. She didn't want to—she's got a mother in town who needs her around. Tisserande's the only good sales job near by. But I don't think she could have taken much more of it. She gets these migraines when she's stressed, and work must have been nothing but stress for her lately." He sighed heavily. "Courtney's our best salesperson too."

"After meeting them all, that's what I would have guessed."

"Yeah, it would have completely ruined our sales to have that rig running it instead of Courtney. It was hard enough running marketing around Melissa. Jake and Blake do okay, but they need some guidance, you know? Sales are supposed to come under the marketing department, so it was frustrating to be blamed for Melissa stoving so many sales up. I can't tell how many times a deal was all lined up, then Paul sent Melissa in and she blew it." He shook his head. "Not her fault really. She just wasn't ready for that level yet." He slowed his rocking pace a little and looked earnestly at Mia. "There's no way Lauren killed Melissa, you know."

"She doesn't seem the type," Mia prevaricated.

"She isn't. Lauren's," he floundered for a word, "good people," Jeremy finally said. "Anyone else would have kicked Paul out long before last night. Man's a drunk. Never liked him. I was just out of college, at my first job in the packing department, when the trustees hired him—hated him from day one. I love Megeso

Point, so I stayed despite him. Working with him was a nightmare, but I guess he had the trustees fooled. And Lauren, until last night."

Mia confidentially leaned toward Jeremy. "Did he try to kill Lauren, and kill Melissa by accident?"

He thought a minute, then shook his head with disappointment, cleaning his glasses again. "Nah, he must have been really into Melissa. Otherwise he'd have let her go over the sales stuff. Paul never steps foot on a boat if he can help it. The rest of us either have boats or take the company boat every chance we get. Paul's a golfer. Spends a ton of time and money on the local course every summer. Calls it networking— hah," He barked out a laugh. "He's there more than at work. Not that we mind."

He went on thoughtfully, "Plus, all he had to do was tell her to wait, and head back with him on the main ferry. Then Lauren would have taken the boat as planned. Melissa would have done that in a second. I was pretty surprised he didn't at the time, to tell the truth." His soft brown eyes looked naked without his glasses, and his rocking had slowed into a regular rhythm. "It's a thought, though. Did someone try to kill Melissa—or Lauren?"

"It's a thought," Mia agreed. She wondered which woman had been the intended victim.

Jake and Blake were on the lawn throwing a frisbee slowly back and forth. Mia stopped a few feet away, smiling at their game. "How are you both doing?"

They stopped their desultory play, and came over

to her. "We're fine. Fine," Jake said.

"Just fine," Blake affirmed.

"I'm so sorry about Melissa," Mia told them. "I know you have a tight knit company so her death must be a dreadful shock."

They looked at each other in silent communication. "Yeah, well," Jake said awkwardly, "She didn't exactly fit into the family."

Blake snickered, "She was more Paul's friend, not ours." He tossed the frisbee from one hand to the other, back and forth.

Mia asked curiously, "Did you know about their affair?"

They looked at each other and shrugged. Jake said, "Yeah, I caught them once in the staff room, at it hot and heavy."

Blake snickered again.

"I figured that was why Melissa always got our sales." Jake shrugged, a quick whole body movement like a dog shaking, and smoothed his blonde hair. "Jeremy wouldn't fire her, so I went to Cynthia and complained." He explained further at the questioning look on Mia's face. "Not about the affair, that wasn't my business, but our sales. She said Melissa's numbers were the best so if anyone went, I would." He shrugged again, "The job's pretty easy and the pay's okay, so I don't want to go. But it pissed me off."

Blake agreed, screwing up his face, "Yeah. Melissa cost me thirty grand last year in commissions." He dropped the frisbee and stooped to pick it up, spinning it in the air and catching it with practiced ease.

Mia said with surprise, "That's a lot of money."

"Yeah," he said dispiritedly. "Seems like with as much as we're selling, there should be more profit." He tossed the frisbee again.

Jake agreed, "Melissa took about that much from my sales too. It got to where I'd just ignore big deals, go after small stuff she wouldn't be interested in. Lots of small commissions are better than big stuff you don't get paid for."

"Yeah," Blake confirmed. "I just didn't bother with anything big enough to hand over."

"And all the small stuff is harder work. Gotta schmooze a lot more people, build a bigger network." Jake wiggled uncomfortably. "Still, we've got access to the company boat for fishing, and my family's got some hunting land up Millinocket way. It's a good life, on the whole."

"It'll be a better one without Melissa and Paul in it," Blake added with a smirk. He spun the frisbee on his finger.

"Paul accused Lauren of killing Melissa?" Mia trailed off in a question.

"No way," Jake said immediately.

Blake confirmed, "No way she'd do that."

"The thing is," Jake explained, "Lauren hasn't really been in the business management part until very recently, like the last few months when she got close to taking control. Paul was hired by the trustees while she was in college, after her parents died. I guess he was good at his job—the company makes money. When she started working at Tisserande full time, she started in the design department. Which is great, people eat up the stuff she does."

"Yeah. She came up with some crazy weird colors last year and they sold like hotcakes." Blake laughed. "Couldn't believe it."

"Yeah. So she hasn't really done the management stuff much yet. She's not a sales type, too shy. She keeps talking about going along on a sales call, but she always puts it off."

"She's not pushy like us," Blake shoved Jake and Jake shoved him back.

They guffawed, then Jake said, "So then she got this idea about reopening the factory here, doing high end stuff,"

Blake cut in, "Spending a ton of company capital. But it's her company. She can spend it how she likes."

"Well, Paul didn't like it." Jake scuffed the ground with his toe, ruffling the grass. "I think it's the first time Lauren's ever pushed back. I've never seen her so certain. Paul would yell and call her stupid in front of everyone in meetings. She'd go all quiet and just say she was building it. I'd say her eyes were opened to what he was really like this past year, if they weren't already."

"Had to have been." Blake emphatically tossed the frisbee. "I mean, if he yelled at her like that in meetings, what'd he do at home?" The two looked at each other knowingly.

"Is that why he had the affair?" Mia asked.

"Paul always got around," Jake winked broadly.

"He was just quieter about it after he married Lauren."

"Didn't want her catching him." Blake spun the frisbee. "After all, he was married to the owner."

"Lots of business trips," Jake shrugged. "Not my business what happened."

"So Melissa would go with him?"

"Yeah, sometimes," Jake's eyes slid away and back. "Sometimes Cynthia."

"Cynthia? Is she having an affair with him?"

"Dunno. Never saw anything." Jake was elaborately noncommittal, eyes flickering to Blake and back. He refocused on Mia, "Look, Lauren's got a lawyer coming, right?"

Mia nodded and looked at her watch. "He should be here any minute. He's coming by the town ferry."

"Good, that's good," Jake meandered. "I'd sure rather work with Lauren than Paul, if you get my drift."

"Needs someone on her side," Blake said.

"Besides Max," They grinned at each other.

"Max?"

"Yeah, Max is her old high school boyfriend, you know." Jake smirked. "He moved back to Megeso Point when his first marriage broke up. His mom still lives in town."

"Yeah, he moved back home because of his mom." Blake sniggered, then got serious. "Max is definitely her enabler on the whole factory thing. They planned the whole thing together before telling anyone else. Paul hates his guts for that, but it's almost impossible getting a good engineer in the middle of nowhere. He can't fire him, even if Lauren would let him. There's no one else who could do his job."

"Yeah, I don't know if she'd have pulled it off if he hadn't helped to plan it."

Mia asked directly, "Are they having an affair?"

"Doubt it," Jake shrugged. "Lauren's married."

"Bet something happens now that Lauren's getting divorced," Blake predicted with a wink.

"I'm not offering you odds on that one," Jake agreed, chuckling.

Mia dropped that intriguing topic. "Who do you think killed Melissa?"

Their eyes both shifted, and they shuffled their feet. Jake finally answered, "We've both been wondering that ourselves. The whole thing doesn't make sense. I still think it could have been an accident. A terrible accident." His blue eyes darted away and back.

She left them, already spreading out to continue their game of frisbee.

Max and Lauren, she thought. They must have been thrown together a lot with the factory project. And it would be difficult for anyone who cared about Lauren to put up with how Paul obviously treated her. Max, who grew up on a lobster boat, must know all there was to know about boat engines. Lauren probably did too, if they'd been dating then. If anyone could turn a boat into a time bomb, it was an engineer who'd grown up on boats. But she couldn't think of any reason Max would have to kill Melissa. She would

108

certainly have been fired after last night, and completely out of the picture. Lauren was divorcing Paul, and she was the one who owned the company. Killing Melissa would have been pointless. If Paul had been scheduled for the boat trip, Max might be her prime suspect. Max had looked like he'd wanted to kill Paul last night. A fight had definitely been a close thing.

But really, even then, why would Max kill Paul? Punch him, yes. Any friend of Lauren's might do that. It sounded like anyone who had worked with Paul might punch him when given the chance. Mia shook her head over Jake's and Blake's lost sales commissions. Melissa had stolen a lot of money from them, if they were telling the truth. And Tisserande Linens must be a very profitable company as well. So a great deal of money was involved around Melissa's death.

Would Max kill Paul, even if he was madly in love with Lauren? Of course not, Mia thought. There was no point after last night's revelation. Lauren would be getting a divorce, and any obstacles to their getting together would be gone. And Paul wasn't the one who had died. Melissa had. She still didn't understand why anyone would want to kill Melissa, except Lauren. And Lauren didn't, Mia searched for a phrase, Lauren didn't seem that emotionally invested in her relationship with Paul at this stage—mostly relieved she'd be free from him. Of course, jealousy usually had very little basis in reality. Lauren might be glad Paul was gone, but still furious with Melissa. Just because she didn't look like she was, didn't mean she wasn't.

Mia saw Paul standing on the point, morosely throwing pebbles off the cliff. She approached him warily, remembering him losing his temper earlier.

"Paul, I just wanted to tell you how sorry I am for your loss."

He turned startled eyes to her, obviously too lost in his thoughts to notice her approach. He cleared his throat. "Um, thanks."

"It's a terrible tragedy," Mia continued.

"You bet it is," Paul told her, his mouth twisting in a snarl. "If the police don't do something to that bitch who did it, I will." He threw a fist sized rock off the cliff and watched it splash far below.

"The police have already questioned you? I think you were next on their list after the hotel manager and me."

"I told them exactly what Lauren had done. She's the one always messing around with boats, not me. Think she doesn't know how to fix one to explode?"

"That makes sense," Mia hedged. "Why would she kill Melissa though? Wouldn't firing her be enough?"

"Jealous bitch," Paul accused vindictively. His polished veneer had worn off. "She'd do anything to get back at me." He pulled back his arm, throwing a baseball size stone onto the rocks below, watching it shatter with satisfaction.

"I thought she was getting a divorce? That's certainly what I understood last night."

"Lauren's sneaky like that," Paul sneered. "Looks

sweet as pie, then screws with everything." He threw another rock, watched it bounce off a boulder, then turned to Mia. "Look, she must have known we were having an affair, and I was going to leave her. I'd stayed in this one horse town long enough." He shuddered at the heavy gray sky on the horizon. "Time to move to California, be in the sun, not this freezing, boring place." He screwed up his face. "Do you know what she does in the evenings? Reads in front of the fire. It's not the eighteen hundreds," he jeered. "Like I'm going to do that my whole life." He snickered. "Not exactly worth coming home for, you know?"

"Why did you marry her, then?"

"She was different in college. More fun. She listened to what I had to tell her. Then she changed. Like this stupid factory thing. She wouldn't listen to me at all on that. Damn stupid idea, getting an antique factory going again. Why go back to the Dark Ages?" He kicked a rock far out into the water. "Like I'm letting that go through. If she's in jail for murder, I'm still the boss."

"I thought she owned the business?"

"She does, in trust. I can't see her running it from prison, though. Her trustees sure aren't going to fire me—they hired me in the first place. Who else would run the show for them?"

"You are the one who's been running it," Mia encouraged thoughtfully.

"Damn right I am. The trustees will have to let me continue. And first thing I'll do is cancel that damn factory." His lips parted slightly in anticipation.

Mia thought keeping his job was wishful thinking on his part. "The factory isn't a good idea?"

Paul scoffed, "It's the stupidest business plan I've ever heard of. Sink a ton of money into a factory that closed a decade ago? Price yourself right out of the market? Like anyone will pay for top quality anything anymore. Halfwitted idea of business." He kicked a rock, and gestured at the hotel. "You know business. There's no way that anyone pays for quality anymore."

Mia's lips thinned, but she manfully demurred, "I see."

"That should have told me she was crazy, right off. Should have had her locked up."

"It's hard to know what someone is going to do," Mia temporized.

"Then she wouldn't have killed Melissa." He kicked out viciously. "I still can't believe that jealous bitch killed Melissa."

"Is there anyone else who could wanted Melissa dead?"

"No, everyone else loved her. Lauren killed her." He punctuated with a hurled rock.

"I understand Melissa was top saleswoman?"

"Too right," Paul agreed heartily. "She'd been saleswoman of the year since she got here." He grinned. "Had what it took, you know?"

"But didn't that cause some jealousy with the other salespeople?"

Paul threw a rock hard at the boulder. It missed and hit the beach below with a clatter. "Look, you have to understand, there's always competition with sales.

That's what it's about." He scoffed, "Heck, we want them competing. That brings in more sales."

"But if Melissa got all the big clients, wouldn't she make all the big sales?" she asked reasonably. "Didn't the others object to that?"

"Who's been telling you that?" Paul looked at Jake and Blake tossing the frisbee, running back and forth like retrievers. "Those two? They couldn't make a big sale if their life depended on it. They just fill in the gaps. Work the little stuff."

"I see," Mia agreed smoothly. "Well, that makes sense. What about Courtney though? She seems like a good salesperson."

"Courtney?" Paul said vaguely. "Oh, yeah, Courtney came in second to Melissa, that's for sure. There were some cat fights between those two but," he shook his head contemptuously, "she wasn't on Melissa's level. Just a lot of bitching about not getting the good accounts." He smirked, "Melissa had what it took. Knew how to pull in the sales." He looked out at the gray ocean. "Courtney wouldn't kill Melissa. It was Lauren."

Mia left Paul throwing rocks at the ocean. It didn't seem to mind.

The sky was still overcast, gray and cold, but guests were walking around the lawn, some hand in hand, enjoying the brief Maine summer. Douglas rattled past in the golf cart, dourly straight behind the wheel next to a small neat man with a permanently worried expression. He must be Lauren's lawyer, Mia thought. She was glad Lauren had called for him before being questioned. The sheriff seemed a bit biased.

She continued strolling between two pink granite boulders at the edge of the lawn and into the sweetly scented balsam fir woods. The path was semi manicured with layers of white pine needles soft beneath her feet. The edges were roughly but clearly defined with tripping hazards removed from the smooth path. Mia approved. There were rough hiking trails on Mount Desert Island for more adventurous guests, but some nice, easy paths around the hotel were perfect for short strolls of the less mobile guests—or a pleasant afternoon stroll. Her feet padded gently, sounds muffled by the soft pine carpet.

This path unfolded in sinuous curves, overlapping each other with signs carefully pointing out distance as well as direction, so you could choose how strenuous a walk you wanted. She slowly made her way down the hill by a smooth switchback and across a little round humped bridge with a tiny burbling stream. Ferns draped the mossy banks. She left the green lushness of the water and climbed up to a shimmering birch stand. Their white peeling trunks shone in the soft light, tiny bright leaves almost glowing. Beneath their trunks, she saw movement and quietly moved closer.

Tina and Andrew Michaud were bending over, baskets in hand, meticulously selecting golden mushrooms from the forest floor.

"Hello," Mia greeted them.

They both stood up, round faces beaming with identical welcoming grins. "Hello, Mia!" Andrew told her, in jolly booming tones. "You would not believe how many mushrooms we've found here. Even better than the other spot we found." With a proud smile, he opened his basket and showed her his treasures.

"Beautiful," Mia told him as she breathed in their woody citrus scent. Fresh chanterelle mushrooms were one of the wonders of the forest. She had never foraged them herself, but she very much appreciated them at the dining table. "I can see we need more local delicacies like this in the restaurant. I had no idea these actually grew on the island."

"You should certainly have these on the menu," Andrew beamed. "People need to appreciate the bounty of this island."

"We're cooking these tonight. We'll certainly share with Chef Ava where we found them," Tina added. She spied another golden treasure in the pale lichen blanket and gently placed it in her basket.

Mia stood for a minute watching them, then noticed a small brown squirrel with a long feathery tail hunched over one of the mushrooms. He circled it speculatively, bending down over it, then gave a mighty heave, uprooting it completely. Placing the mushroom over his shoulder like a tremendous bright yellow umbrella, he hurried off. Mia stifled a laugh.

She stood watching the Michauds for another minute, hoping to see another squirrel adding to his winter larder. None came and she left quietly, without the Michauds even noticing. It was nice to see guests who apparently hadn't even seen the explosion. It certainly hadn't worried them if they had.

Lauren greeted Harvey Thompson, her lawyer, with a quick hug and relieved sigh. "Uncle Harvey, I'm so glad you're here. This is a mess."

He endured the hug with good grace, barely grimacing at all. Harvey was very obviously not a hugger, but he'd known Lauren since she was an impetuous little girl who gave him unasked for hugs, coming to his office with her parents. She'd been a polite little girl, he remembered, sitting quietly with a book in the anteroom while he talked with her parents. He had approved.

Later, she had been a gawky, serious teenager, coming to his office all alone, after her parents' deaths. She had been determined to do everything precisely as they would have wanted. He remembered her looking at him seriously and saying, "I need to get this right, Uncle Harvey. Everyone is depending on me." He had approved.

He had not approved of her marriage to Paul. The trustees Lauren's parents had chosen appointed

116

Paul Baker, with a complete lack of oversight and vetting, in his considered opinion. He had been outvoted.

He did not approve of the way Paul Baker had run Tisserande Linens, nor did he think Lauren's parents would have approved. When Lauren announced her upcoming marriage to Paul, saying warmheartedly, "Of course you'll come to the wedding, Uncle Harvey," he had kept his carefully schooled face blank and made certain her prenuptial agreement was iron clad.

When Paul Baker had objected to the agreement, Harvey had been firm, stating it was necessary because the company was still in trust for Lauren. That had not been precisely the reason for the rigorous prenup. When her marriage was announced, Harvey Thompson had foreseen Lauren's phone call early this morning, and planned accordingly in the prenup. He had considered Lauren's parents not only his clients, but two of his closest friends. Lauren was the closest thing he had to a daughter. He would see to it that Paul Baker did not steal another penny of Lauren's money.

He perched himself precisely on the edge of the chair in Lauren's hotel room, made a preliminary, "Ah hum," smoothed his thinning hair back from his high forehead, and got down to business.

Cynthia's desk in her hotel room was hidden under neatly stacked papers, but she still couldn't find all the information she wanted for her report. Why Lauren couldn't have planned a working weekend at the corporate office, she didn't know. Why it was considered fun to work on a trip, she didn't know either. When she was working in her office, it was so much easier to have all her files ready around her, neatly tabulated and in the proper drawers. Stacks of paper, she looked at her burdened desk and sighed, were so messy.

Most information was digital now, of course, but Cynthia always kept paper backups for everything. She had never trusted digital, even if all her work was done on her computer and stored in the cloud. The cloud, she thought, just meant other people's computers. Digital documents could be altered so easily, and there was no way to prove they'd ever been anything else. She always kept the originals as backups for anything she felt important.

Especially with the mess Paul made of the company in the last few years. After they had sent all their production offshore, the big stores continually asked for lower prices. There was always a competitor waiting in the wings who could beat their price. And the price was the only important thing. To stay in the game, they lowered prices. As the prices went down, the quality went down too. It had to. They cut corners, laid off more people, contracted with cheaper factories. The problem was they couldn't keep that up forever. The requests to lower prices were endless. Soon

Tisserande sheets would be as disposable as toilet paper.

So Paul had told her to keep one set of accounting books for him and one for Lauren and her trustees. It wasn't really dishonest, she told herself. He was the CEO, after all. If she didn't do what her boss said, she'd be fired.

The numbers added up to the same totals. The online and small store sales selling their better quality linens supported the cheap big box store items instead of the other way around. What did it matter where the money came from? The totals all came to the same thing.

With the spreadsheets she'd laid out, no one would ever guess there were two sets of books. Until today, when she'd admitted the juggling act to everyone. And put the blame squarely on Paul, who'd caused it all.

She'd been terrified what the auditors might see when they went through the books as Lauren's trusteeship ended. It all depended on just how detailed their audit was. Previous audits hadn't been a problem, so there was no real reason to think the next one would be. However, she had a feeling the audit would be much more rigorous after Melissa's death, especially if the police were involved. No matter, she'd put the blame firmly on Paul, where it rightfully should be. He was the CEO, after all.

The money the books showed should be in the bank, though she did wonder just how much money Paul had been slipped to put all production offshore or do those cheap linen deals. She had a feeling he'd made more in under the table deals in his factory choices than he'd ever told her about. Why else would he have insisted the big markets were the profitable ones?

Well, now she'd admitted making reports that expressed Paul's wishes, at his request. If she hadn't done as he asked, she'd have been fired. He was the boss, after all. It wasn't her fault.

Cynthia slowly sipped her tea, trying to calm her nerves. Her mind was racing. What a horrible day it had been. She fingered her bright bead bracelet, remembering she had bought it last year on the Caribbean company trip. She wished again Lauren had either stayed home and worked or gone back to the tropics with a fun company vacation. Combining work and vacation was such a ridiculous idea.

Melissa's death had completely shocked her. Cynthia still felt shaky when she thought about it. Who would have thought Melissa would ever pilot a boat, let alone die on one?

She had disliked Melissa intensely, but had been forced to work with her, even to fight to keep her on. Her tangerine colored lips twisted in disgust.

Melissa had been one of the stupidest people she'd ever run across, Cynthia thought. She didn't think Paul would have trusted Melissa with anything she might blab about, but Cynthia thought he'd use her death to his advantage if he could.

Yes, Paul would use that slut's death to his advantage. She began to think how she could use it for hers.

Jeremy smiled up at Courtney as she ventured out to the porch. "Take a chair," he offered, pushing his glasses up.

Courtney sat down and leaned back, letting her head rest on the soft cushion. "It's been a crazy day, hasn't it?"

"I still can't believe it," Jeremy agreed. "Doesn't seem real."

She rubbed her temples. "I can't either. Just seems like a nightmare."

"Getting one of your headaches?"

"Yeah," she said dully.

"Want me to go get your meds?"

She looked up at him gratefully. "Yeah, could you?" She grimaced. "I don't want to miss anything but I don't want an all day migraine either." She handed him her key. "It's on the bathroom counter in a pill bottle. Rizatriptan."

"No problem." He bounded away on his mission and was back almost immediately, pill bottle in hand.

She gulped it down with some tea. "Thanks, Jeremy. That'll make it go away soon."

"Ayuh," he mumbled. "It's been a day, that's for

sure." He looked at her with concern, soft brown eyes misty behind his glasses.

"I'll get started on the sales ideas soon, don't worry," she reassured him. "Just as soon as this calms down." She rubbed her temples, brows furrowed.

"Don't worry about that now, Courtney. Just relax, have a scone." He passed her a plate piled high. "I know perfectly well you've been dreaming up sales ideas since Lauren came up with the new factory. You'll do fine." He smiled at her kindly. "No one's up to much today, after that." He gave a quick, sharp nod at the ocean. "Just a matter of going through the motions so we keep swimming."

Courtney burst out, "I feel so bad about the whole thing. I really didn't like Melissa, but—"

"Well, she did steal all your best sales," Jeremy commiserated, rocking gently.

"Yeah, but to end like that." Courtney sighed, rubbing her temples. "Any other place, she'd have learned not to poach. Or at least do it more discreetly," she added with a wry smile.

"How's your mom doing?" Jeremy changed the subject.

"She's okay. About the same," Courtney said automatically.

"That's good, then." Jeremy looked out into the gray fog, obviously thinking of something to talk about besides murder. "I wish we'd gone to the Caribbean again."

"Me too," she agreed with feeling. "Splashing in the water, lying on the sand and not worrying about a thing." She smiled at him, deep brown eyes plaintive. "That'd be nice."

"After the factory is up and running, we should plan another trip." Jeremy looked at her out of the corner of his eye. "You and I might go, even if Lauren doesn't plan it."

"Middle of the winter, when our eyeballs are freezing up," Courtney suggested with a shy smile.

"Absolutely." Jeremy smiled back at her. "Maybe it won't be such a bad summer, either."

Courtney took a bite of her scone. Her face was growing less pinched as she relaxed. "Summer here is the best. It was the thing I missed most when I lived in the city."

"I've never wanted to live anywhere else," Jeremy said. He added quickly, "Wouldn't mind traveling a bit, though."

"Me too. I mean, I travel for work, but I never really see much of where I go. Too busy working. Be nice to relax and explore a bit. Go out for dinner without clients." She added with a bite in her voice, "Now Melissa definitely saw the night life."

"I'll bet," Jeremy agreed with derision.

"I wouldn't even see her at client meetings half the time. She'd be out, doing who knows what." Courtney's lips pursed tightly. "I still can't believe she's gone, just like that."

"Don't think about it," Jeremy suggested. "There's nothing we can do about it."

"I guess." Courtney looked out where the boat had disappeared. She took a bite of her scone, then crumbled it onto her plate. "Maybe I'd better go lie down for a bit, after all."

"I think you should," Jeremy looked at her with concern. "Want me to walk you?" He started to stand up.

"No, no, I'll be fine," Courtney rose stiffly and slowly walked inside.

Jeremy remained with a worried look on his face, slowly rocking.

Lauren was even more glad she had Harvey at her side as she entered the office. Chief White growled, "Sit down. So you're Lauren Tisserande Baker, are you?"

"Yes." She carefully arranged her pants legs and tried not to shake. Harvey had told her not to volunteer anything whatsoever.

Chief White just looked pugnaciously at her, ready for a battle. It was an effort for her not to fill that empty, censorious silence.

Finally he barked, "My aunt worked at Tisserande. Forty years. You laid her off when you closed the factory. Not even a severance check after all that time." He glared at her in personal accusation. "Forty years."

Lauren's heart fell. She said nothing. There was nothing she could say.

Harvey stepped in for her, "I believe you'll find Mr. Paul Baker, the CEO, was in complete charge of the factory from the time Ms. Tisserande's parents died until later this week when Ms. Tisserande's parents' trust is completed. Ms. Tisserande has no say in business operations until this week, when the trust is dissolved."

"Huh. Your name's Tisserande, isn't it?"

"Yes," Lauren kept to the monosyllable.

"Your name on the company sign, then." He scratched angrily at the paper. "So, Ms. Melissa Hathway was having an affair with your husband."

"Yes," Lauren carefully agreed. There wasn't much point in denying it.

"You found out last night and decided to divorce him," he stated.

Lauren nodded agreement.

"When did you decide to murder her instead?" the chief barked. His beady eyes avidly watched for her reaction.

Harvey quickly held up a hand. "I advise my client not to answer that question."

Lauren felt her palms sweating through her pants legs. She carefully smoothed the fabric and said nothing.

"Fine, but she'll have to answer it eventually." Chief White growled. "Let's see if she's in the mood to answer this one. Why did you offer Ms. Hathway the boat?"

Lauren looked at Harvey. He nodded. She drew in a deep breath, forcing her voice not to shake. "Ms.

Hathway was causing a scene in the hotel lobby. She wished to leave immediately and no boat was available." She looked at Harvey. "I realized there were several phone calls I needed to make regarding my divorce, and I could make them most effectively from my room here."

"Phone calls?" Chief White demanded.

"To my lawyer to start paperwork, my bank and other lines of credit, people at Tisserande Linens."

"Still have some people you haven't fired there, huh?" He dug his pen in the paper as he wrote, scratching at the paper. "Why did you go back to the boat?"

"I had left my laptop bag on the boat. I wanted to get that." Lauren smiled ruefully. "I thought with how Melissa was acting she'd have thrown it in the ocean."

Harvey frowned at her, and she wiped her smile off, leaving her face carefully blank.

"So Ms. Hathway was angry with you?"

"She was," Lauren considered. "She scratched my arm with her nails." She displayed the claw marks, still red on her arm. "She seemed desperate to get off the island."

"Maybe she was scared of you," Chief White accused, unimpressed by the scratch marks. "Maybe she wanted to get away from you."

Harvey tried to cut in, but Lauren was faster. "No, she was not scared of me," she stated evenly. "She had no reason to be frightened of me."

"Then why was she in such a hurry to leave?" he

rejoined.

"I don't know. I just didn't want her making a scene." Lauren smoothed her pants.

"Why were you so quick to ask for a divorce?" he barked.

Lauren sighed and looked at Harvey. He nodded. "I caught him with Ms. Hathway. Surely that's reason enough?"

"Not to most women. Most women want to keep their husbands around unless they have another one lined up. They want more reason than maybe just a little misunderstanding to go through a divorce. Are you sure you were the one who wanted a divorce? Not your husband?" Chief White wrote in a heavy black scrawl. "Right. Don't leave the island." He glared at her, then looked down in clear dismissal.

Lauren left the room without a second glance, Harvey trailing her. She started to speak when they were in the hall, but Harvey frowned at her and motioned upstairs. They silently took the elevator, Lauren staring straight ahead, keeping her eyes fastened on a knot in the smooth wood panel of the door.

When she got to her room and closed the door behind her, she collapsed on the sofa, crying, her head in her hands. Harvey awkwardly patted her shoulder a few times, then sat down to wait her out, paging through his briefcase. After a few minutes, she stopped crying. What was the point?

She went to the bathroom, scrubbed her face raw with icy cold water and brushed her hair. She came out, picked up a pen and paper, and asked, "So what do I do now?"

6

Around the Island

Mia returned to the hotel at lunchtime, pleasantly anticipating a hearty meal after her long morning walk around the island. The first thing she heard as she walked in was Kayla reassuring guests lunch would be served soon. The doors to the main dining room were still closed, and hungry looking guests prowled the lounge area in search of sustenance. The trays of cookies had been reduced to crumbs. Some of the guests seemed to be contemplating the meager morsels. It was not a welcome sight for a hotel owner.

Kayla sighted Mia's entrance and rushed over, a worried expression on her normally cheerful face. Her words spilled out in a rush, "Ms. Mia, the Acadia dining room isn't open for lunch yet. The doors are still locked. It's fifteen minutes late opening already.

Joseph's over on the mainland, the assistant managers are being questioned by the police, and Chef Ava went to Bangor to purchase supplies early this morning. I can't leave the desk, and I can't get hold of the sous chef or the kitchen—no one is answering the phones. Would you please find out what's going on in the kitchen?" Her forcibly calm tone held desperation.

Mia wasted no time, but quickly strode down the service hallway to the main restaurant's kitchen. She arrived to complete chaos.

The Michauds had taken over one of the main counters, spreading their chanterelles over the entire stainless steel counter in obvious pride at their haul. The sous chef, his tall white hat crumpled and lopsided, was gesturing wildly at the oblivious couple, clearly ordering them to leave his kitchen.

The sous chef was definitely getting the worst of the altercation. His round face glowed beet red and his balled fists shook in impotent fury. His voice was hoarse from cursing the Michauds in French. They remained oblivious, too interested in carefully sorting their precious mushrooms by size and quality.

The rest of the kitchen team ringed around the drama, ignoring the petty details of cooking food and lunch preparation. It had been a disturbing and stressful day. Finally, here was some entertainment to break the tension. Their faces were rapt with glee, watching their sous chef inanely bellow at the hotel guests.

Mia's icy voice cut through the crowd. "What is the meaning of this?"

The white-jacketed herd started and sprang apart, still wrapped up in the show.

"Is something burning?" Mia's voice dripped with disgust as she sniffed the air and a junior chef ran to his smoke filled station.

Another chef stepped back, then walked with portly dignity to his station. A prep cook hurriedly chopped carrots while another chef cursed at him in rapid fire French, avoiding Mia's eye. Servers rushed out of the kitchen to prepare the restaurant. The kitchen returned to normal, except for the sous chef standing in the middle of it with his hands clenched into fists and his dark red face. He stopped yelling, cheeks puffing to a halt as he ran out of breath. The Michauds didn't even notice, benignly grading their treasures.

Throwing up his hands in despair, the sous chef took off his apron, threw it on the floor and marched out through the restaurant. Mia watched him leave with her mouth open, aghast at his unprofessional behavior.

She looked at the Michauds, happily sorting mushrooms on the main prep counter for a minute more, then spoke in a penetrating voice cutting through the bustle of the kitchen. "Mr. and Mrs. Michaud, you can't use that counter."

They looked up at her, startled at the interruption. "It was empty," Andrew Michaud told her, spreading his hands.

"It was cleared for the lunch prep. You can't use it at lunchtime. My chefs don't have a place to prepare meals."

"You told us we could use the kitchen here," Andrew accused. He looked with plaintive eyes at his golden treasure spread across the counter.

"Yes, but this is clearly not the time or place." She looked at the door the chef had marched through. "I believe my sous chef just quit."

"That man clearly doesn't appreciate gourmet food," Tina told her, shaking her head sorrowfully.

Mia shrugged noncommittally, examining the chaos around the kitchen. The burned pan clanged into the sink and a prep cook furiously chopped onions to replace the charred contents. She looked at the Michauds. "I'll have your mushrooms carefully packed and you set up in an appropriate cooking location by dinner time. For now, please go to the restaurant for lunch. I'll let you know where you can cook dinner when I've worked that out."

"Not just any mushrooms. Chanterelles," Andrew said, greedily eyeing them with hunger.

"Absolutely. Please don't worry about your chanterelles. I'll take care of them." Mia ushered them out of the kitchen and into the restaurant with a firm hand as they gazed back longingly.

The kitchen team studiously avoided her eyes as she came back into the room. Pans clanged and knives chopped furiously, everyone looking as busy as they possibly could. "All right, is everyone back on track now? Can we let the guests into the dining room? There are hungry guests waiting to eat outside those doors right now," her voice rose imperiously.

The hostess stopped busily organizing napkins and ran to the doors to unlock them. Two waiters followed her at controlled sprints, bearing iced water jugs. The sous chef's station remained empty.

She sighed and firmly tied an apron around her waist. Her lunch would have to wait. "What do you need?" she asked the tall chef manning the central station. His lean frame bent with nurturing care over his cooking, full attention on his pan.

His dark eyes darted to her, then returned quickly to his frying pan. "Everything's under control except the specials. Chef Ava usually prepares those and the sous chef takes care of them when she's off." He glanced quickly up at a whiteboard. "Let me see, lunch is less formal than dinner, naturally, so we can manage." He gave her a brief nod of dismissal, turning back to his pan, deftly adding a sprinkle of pepper.

Mia looked at the board, planning. "I'll make the lobster ravioli. It's one of my favorites. And the spring greens with grilled salmon salad." She nodded to him, "You continue with the scallops in béarnaise sauce. That needs your full attention."

He looked at her, aghast at her invasion, "You can't just..." he broke off in confusion, delicately stirring his béarnaise sauce. She was the boss and it had been a very long day.

"I think you will find that I can," Mia calmly informed him. She nodded to the prep chef obviously making the pasta sheets for the ravioli. "I'll need those in five minutes."

Nothing was ready yet at the sous chef's station.

133

She quickly grabbed butter, checked the lobster broth was simmering and diced shallots into tiny pieces. She simmered the onions in buttery broth, adding the lobster meat and tiny hints of tarragon.

She saw the tall chef's dark eyes constantly flicking to her station, judging her skill. Several times he almost said something, but visibly held it back. He didn't hold back on the other chefs, Mia noticed. He'd call to not forget the thyme to one chef, then tell another to pull his pan off the heat, quick. The kitchen ebbed and flowed, always moving around the tall chef.

Mia smiled as her sauce came together. The prep chef came running with sheets of fresh pasta laid out on a tray. Mia floured the counter, placed the pasta on it, then neatly scooped small balls of filling onto the pasta and painted the edges with egg wash. She placed a fresh sheet on top, sealed the edges and gently cut the fragile shapes apart.

When her first order came in, she carefully simmered the ravioli in a rich mix of butter and lobster broth. She smiled at the other chef's nervous eyes as she elegantly plated the delicacy. A few wisps of tarragon leaves scattered on top, and she placed it on the shelf for the waiter. She saw the chef relax his shoulders, relieved that she wouldn't let the restaurant down. He gave her a darting smile, then continued his frantic stirring of béarnaise sauce with one hand, while turning scallops carefully in a pan with the other.

She continued simmering and plating ravioli while grilling salmon on the other side of her station. Each salmon steak had precisely placed scorch marks, as she'd been taught in her culinary school classes. She whipped up a quick honey mustard dressing and tossed the salad greens in it, barely coating them. It was a classic combination, but always delicious if done well. Nothing wrong with the classics. The salad mix was interesting, with tiny spring pea shoots and delicate miners lettuce mixed in with the more expected baby butter lettuces.

An hour went by with her hardly noticing anything but her job. She only vaguely saw prep cooks running to different stations, the tall chef checking out her work and the waiters bustling in and out of the double doors. Like all good restaurants, the dining area was a peaceful oasis, but under the surface, the kitchen was a frantic race.

When the last order came in, she plated it with relief and stretched deeply, reaching her arms up toward the ceiling, feeling stiff muscles relax. It had been a while since she'd cooked like this. Most of the noise in the kitchen was now from dishes washing. The bright cymbal of pots being cleaned rang throughout the room.

The tall chef came over to her. "So, you did pretty well." He held out a hand, "I'm Carlos, by the way."

Mia shook it. "I'm Mia."

"Mia Spinel, yes. You own this hotel." It was a statement, not a question.

Mia corrected him, "My family owns the hotel."

"But you've worked in a restaurant before."

She corrected his statement again. "I've stepped in to help before. I've worked in hotels for a long

135

time." She gave Carlos a quick grin. "I never know what I'll be doing the next day."

"That is true." He was thoughtful, his long arms hanging by his side, with bony wrists poking out of his white shirt sleeves. "This has been a day, that's for sure."

"It certainly has," Mia said fervently. "I don't want to see another like this one."

"So, you want to eat?" Carlos asked her diffidently.

She nodded, suddenly starving. "I would indeed."

He led her to a big stainless steel table. Most of the chefs were gathered around it. There was a strict hierarchy in the kitchen, with prep chefs and waiters at one end and the ranked chefs seated in honor at the opposite side, along with the sommelier. Carlos and Mia sat at the head of the table. "What would you like, Ms. Spinel?"

"Do call me Mia, please." She thought a minute and smiled, cocking her head to one side. "I do hope the lobster ravioli is on the menu again tomorrow. I never did get more than a taste and it's one of my favorites."

He smiled down at her. "And it seems that the chef preparing it has stepped away."

"What about a simple smoked salmon sandwich? I think you had that paired with a baguette?" That would be quick for the tired team to pull together, she thought.

He nodded in easy understanding, crooking a long finger for a prep cook who came running.

136

As she waited, Mia looked around the kitchen. It was clean and orderly again. She'd been disappointed at the sous chef's meltdown, but pleased with Carlos's performance. She looked forward to discussing both with Chef Ava.

All around the table, quiet descended as food was served. She bit into her sandwich with pleasure. The crisp shell of the French bread contrasted perfectly with the smoked salmon filling. It tasted even better than she thought it would. Hunger was always the best sauce. She smiled in simple happiness.

Chef Carlos broke the silence. "So, it's been a long day."

"It has." Mia delicately brushed crumbs from her lap.

"Quite a tragedy today."

One of the busboys cut in, "When I got here, there were police all over the docks."

The headwaiter, Jackson, swallowed hard. "I couldn't believe it. A woman killed like that. Here." He shook his head in disgust, then took another crisp bite of his sandwich.

The busboy continued, "And we take the boat home every night."

Jackson added, "Everyone but Carlos."

Carlos clarified, "I have my own boat. I like the ocean at night. Very calming after a busy day."

"I can see that," Mia agreed. She paused a minute, then added, "Did anyone see anything last night?"

The busboy chimed in, "Like someone rigging

the boat to explode?"

"Or anything else that looked odd."

Faces looked expectantly around the table. Mia smiled encouragingly.

The busboy cheerfully rambled on. "Wow, that'd be something. We could have seen the murderer putting a bomb on the boat? Do you really think it happened at night?"

He showed no signs of stopping until Jackson gave him a quelling glance and a sharp, "Nick!" He shut his mouth, then shoveled a huge bite of potato into his mouth.

Mia explained, "I have no idea when the boat was rigged to explode. I wondered if it happened last night or this morning."

Jackson's thin hands held his water glass carefully. "The restaurant team living off the island go back to Southwest Harbor in two shifts, one for the main restaurant team, such as the chefs and busboys," he glared again at the red headed boy who grinned back with bulging cheeks. "That leaves at eleven every night. One for bar hospitality and night kitchen at two o'clock in the morning."

"That's late, but not as bad as some places," Mia commented. "So a boat is continually shuttling the hospitality team on and off the island?"

"It's not nearly as late as some hotels with a more active night life. Guests are out exploring nature all day, so most are asleep by midnight, at the latest," Jackson smiled. "There are three drivers we contract with. They constantly move the hospitality team and supplies on and off the island each shift."

"Why didn't Kayla suggest Melissa take that?"

Jackson smiled thinly. "I doubt Ms. Hathway would have wanted to take that boat. It's a bit rough and ready. Full of supply boxes and the hotel team."

"I see." Mia thought a minute. "But it still departs from the hotel dock, so that's a few times someone might have seen something. What time does the first morning boat arrive?"

"At five in the morning."

"So that's a very tight window for sabotage."

Carlos said slowly, "I don't think it would take very long to sabotage a boat, if you knew what you were doing." His dark eyes darted up to meet hers, then moved quickly away.

Mia patted her mouth with her napkin and stood up. "Thank you so much for that lovely meal. I think I'll escape before you find more work for me."

They all laughed. Mia wasn't surprised when Carlos walked with her, saying, "Chef Ava will be back soon, so you don't need to worry about us being short a chef." He smiled down at her. "We won't make you work all the time you're here."

Mia told him with a reassuring smile, "I have no concern at all that you'd be able to handle the kitchen with a little lead time."

He gave her a quick smile. "The Michauds, now, I have an idea, if you would permit?"

"Absolutely. They have been frustrating, but I also sympathize with a couple that likes to cook for their vacation."

"Yes, I agree, but not in the hotel kitchen. I have a much better place for them."

"Good." Mia looked at the tall, competent chef. He seemed uncertain, still wanting to say something. "Is there something else worrying you?"

"A little," Carlos said. "I enjoy piloting my boat home at night, as we were saying. If the weather's bad, I go in the service boat because it is bigger against the rough seas. Otherwise, I take my own."

She nodded encouragingly.

"Last night, when I went to the dock, I thought I heard someone on the dock. Running footsteps, then silence. I thought it was teenagers on the dock. So I waved my flashlight around." He shrugged his shoulders. "I saw nothing. But plenty of boats to hide behind, on the dock. As I pushed off, I saw a single figure running up the hill from the dock." He smiled thinly, "With kids, there are usually at least two."

"What time was this?" asked Mia intently.

"About midnight. I'm not sure exactly." He shrugged again. "I leave when the kitchen is done for the night. I don't look at the clock."

"Yes," Mia said slowly. "But the figure was on the dock, not the Harrier?"

"Yes. I haven't mentioned it to the police because of that. Someone on the dock at night is not unusual. Should I tell them?"

She looked at him, "I think you should. They should know someone was on the dock late last night. Would you like me to come with you? Or get a hotel lawyer to go with you?" she added, more practically.

Most people didn't like to talk with the police, innocent or not.

He gave her a sudden, bright smile. "No, I think I can handle it. I'll go now, before dinner prep." They went out the service door into the hotel, and he strode off, long legs anxious to finish the task at hand.

Mia nodded in approval, then slowly walked down the hall. She needed a quiet place to think.

Mia nestled in the green velvet wing chair, next to the fire in the little room off the library. It had been a long day and it wasn't over yet. She wondered what had really happened to Melissa. And why Melissa? It certainly hadn't been just a boat accident. Apart from the potential hotel liability, she thought, shuddering a little, she knew Douglas took excellent care of the boats. He would never have permitted any maintenance slackness. Boats didn't just blow up. It must have a deliberate murder.

She considered Melissa. She hadn't taken to the woman, but she had seemed very young still, much younger than her biological age. She'd known a few grasping personality types that settled down once they felt they'd made it. After they didn't feel they had anything to prove, they could be themselves, not just a selfish facade. They no longer continually tried to pull one over on the world. Of course, most people of that type also usually decided they wanted bigger and better things, endlessly. They could never appreciate what they actually had, just what they wanted to have next. They continually grabbed at what belonged to others, like spoiled toddlers.

Melissa would never have the chance to grow into a considerate adult now. It was doubtful she would have, but that choice had been stolen from her. Mia sighed at the waste of a young life.

What had Melissa wanted? She had seemed to want Paul. Why did she want him, really? Did she want Paul or Paul's money? Was she trying to take Paul from Lauren for selfish reasons? But Melissa had worked for Tisserande, so she knew Lauren was the actual owner and Paul's fortune was determined by Lauren. So a permanent, open relationship with Paul would be impossible, unless Lauren was dead. An affair couldn't be hidden forever, nor would it give Melissa the emotional and financial security she had clearly craved.

Paul hadn't been emotionally available. And he didn't have money on his own. So why had Melissa wanted Paul?

Mia briefly considered Melissa blowing up the boat by accident while trying to rig it to kill Lauren on the return journey, but quickly gave that option up. There just hadn't been time, and she'd been in full view. There was no chance for a suicide, even if Mia had believed Melissa wanted to take that final step. If

Melissa had been a killer, she would have sabotaged the boat once she'd reached the town dock, where Lauren would be picking it up later. No, Melissa was the victim, poor woman. What had she wanted out of life that lead to her murder?

Or had someone wanted Lauren dead and Melissa had just been in the wrong boat?

As Mia sipped her hot apple cider, Courtney came in the room, cradling her laptop in a polished leather bag. She started when she saw Mia, clearly expecting the small, tucked away room to be empty. Mia welcomed her in with a smile, concealing her avid anticipation. Courtney seemed too shy to be a saleswoman, but she had a feeling the woman had hidden depths.

Courtney ventured inward with a tentative smile, thin shoulders slumped with exhaustion. "Hi, Mia. How are you?"

"I'm good, considering the day we've had. How are you holding up? It must be quite a shock to have your coworker die so unexpectedly."

"It was." Courtney shivered a little, sitting down abruptly as if her legs had given up under the strain. One thin hand stroked the other sleeve, hugging herself for comfort. "It's pretty awful." Her sallow face paled at the memory of the boat explosion. "Such a terrible way to die."

"Were you close to Melissa? I know you're both on the sales team, so you must have worked together often." Mia knew Courtney must have disliked Melissa, at the least, for stealing so many commissions, but she was curious as to what the woman would say.

"Well, no, not really." Courtney shrugged her shoulders in a tight noncommittal wiggle. "Of course, with sales we're on the road a lot."

"I heard she stole some of your sales," Mia bluntly prompted.

Courtney's laugh was brittle. "She did indeed. There never was a sale she didn't try to take credit for." She paused a minute, her brown eyes luminous behind their dark lashes. "Did Jake and Blake tell you that?" She sighed heavily, "It doesn't matter. Everyone knew. It's not like I didn't complain every chance I got. I didn't have anything to hide."

"Did everyone know about Melissa and Paul's affair?"

"Well, I guessed," Courtney's long fingers twined together, then she shoved back a stray lock of dark hair. "I didn't know. I didn't want to know." She continued, "You can't assume someone's cheating just by how they treat someone else. Besides, it wasn't unusual for Paul to be," she paused to search for the right word, "inappropriate." She looked down at the floor, obviously not wanting to elaborate.

Mia wondered how many passes Paul had made at Courtney, and whether she'd ever responded to them. She sympathized, "I see. Well, it's not the sort of thing you would want to tell Lauren in any case."

"No, I wouldn't want to be responsible for breaking up anyone's marriage, that's for sure." Courtney pulled her laptop out and placed it on a nearby table. She twisted her narrow lips together.

"You know, I think Cynthia was as upset as Lauren to learn about the affair." She quickly glanced sidelong to see Mia's reaction.

Mia, thinking furiously behind her casually friendly face, asked bluntly, "Did Paul have an affair with Cynthia?"

Courtney shook her head halfheartedly. "I never saw anything definite. I mean, he flirts with everyone." She shrugged awkwardly and slumped down in her seat, eyes hiding behind her dark hair. "I don't know. But I wouldn't be surprised." She rolled her eyes expressively. "I saw her coming out of his room a few minutes ago, looking pretty pleased with herself, considering everything that's been happening. I don't want to know more, if you know what I mean." She shook her head. "Melissa gone and Lauren in charge means I might like my job again, so I don't want to rock the boat."

Mia nodded with understanding and sipped her hot cider slowly, sure there was more Courtney hadn't said. She wondered if Courtney knew Paul was a philanderer from personal experience or observation. She had a shrewd guess which and wondered just how vindictive that might make Courtney.

Courtney smiled uncertainly, "You know, maybe you could help me?" She opened her laptop, looking over it at Mia with hopeful eyes.

"What can I do to help?" Mia asked curiously.

"Well, I'm putting together a sales plan for the new line. Max says the factory will start production in eight months, so..."

"Orders are placed a year in advance in the hotel industry, and you need to get the word out and orders coming in. I know," Mia finished for her.

"I have some awesome samples Max did, so I can show people the actual product. But I'd like to know a little more about what luxury features hotels are looking for when they buy higher end linens. From the management point of view." Courtney looked expectantly at her, sweeping her lush dark hair back from her face. Her attitude was completely different now she was back in her comfort zone. She sat up straighter, and seemed more alive somehow, like she'd closed the door on Melissa's death.

"Hmm, let me see." Mia took a long drink of her hot cider, savoring the spicy aroma. "Most importantly, I want my guests to have the best possible experience when they stay with us. Obviously good sheets are an important part of a perfect night's sleep. Our hotels always have our own laundry on site enabling us to iron our sheets so they're crisp and perfectly smooth. Sending laundry out simply isn't good enough. It's worth the extra effort to do it right."

Courtney nodded, tapping on her keyboard. "How long do you expect sheets to last?"

"Well, there are always accidental tears and damage, but they should last a minimum of three to six months. One Maine season, here." She smiled at Courtney. "A less detail oriented hotel chain would keep them around six months to a year, but when ours have any wear whatsoever on them, we donate them so our guests always have perfect sheets."

146

"Three months," Courtney tapped thoughtfully. She flashed a smile at Mia. "I always prefer older sheets that are soft, myself."

"I think hotel sheets should be a little different from home sheets. A little special. Very few people have the time to iron sheets at home any more."

Courtney burst into unrestrained laughter, "I know I don't."

"No one does," Mia chuckled. "Well, let's see. Hotel sheets are usually white. Duvets and accessories are usually colored to coordinate with the room decor, of course, but hotel laundry is always easiest on white sheets. They're not just clean, but they look clean. They have to almost sparkle."

"I remember my mom always had white sheets hanging on the laundry line all summer long. They smelled so good."

"Sun bleaching is the very best. And they turn out so crisp with a breeze drying them." Mia said, remembering pulling fresh sheets off the laundry line when she'd been a child. Sleeping in sun dried sheets had been like sleeping in the very essence of summer. "I wish we could do that in hotels, but it would be impossible."

"I can see why you can't. A lot of work." Courtney sighed, looking into the fire sadly. "I wish my mom still felt up to doing that."

Mia asked hesitantly, "Is she sick?"

"Yeah, she's in chemo. Cancer. That's why I'm working at Tisserande, so I can live with her. My dad's gone. This way I can be home when she needs me."

Her narrow face crumpled into painful exhaustion, with more lines than her age. She rubbed her throbbing temple with one delicate finger. "Jeremy's been good about working with the schedule I need right now. Always lets me take off, or come home quickly when she has chemo or an emergency. He's even driven her to the hospital himself when I had a flight delayed. Talk about a great boss." She smiled a little and shrugged. "There aren't many jobs left in Megeso Point, and I like most of the people at the company. It was worth dealing with Paul to stay with my mom."

Mia said with sympathy, "I'm glad you can be there for her."

"Yeah, me too." Courtney's dark brown eyes filled with tears, and she blinked them away quickly.

Mia looked into the fire, giving Courtney time to recover. She changed the subject after a minute. "I suppose hotels and homes want different types of sheets. You must have to do separate sales campaigns for each."

Courtney slid gratefully back to the topic of work. "Yes, and different campaigns for each grade of sheet. I mean," she gestured around, "this is a high end hotel. You want something really different from a basic hotel. Something special, like you said."

Mia laughed, "We do indeed."

"And home is a completely different game. Just on texture, some people want crisp sheets and some want limp ones," Courtney made a face. "I hate limp sheets, myself."

148

"Whatever the customer wants is right."

"Exactly," Courtney warmed to her topic. "And some want white, but the crazy colors and patterns Lauren mixes are selling like hotcakes, especially in high end residential markets."

"Lauren mixes them?" Mia asked curiously.

"Oh, yeah, she has a mad scientist lab with all the chemicals and everything." Courtney giggled. "It started out a pristine white and now there's random splotches of our latest dye colors all over it. The room looks like an artist's canvas. You can't scrub it clean. I know what colors I'll be selling in a few months by the latest spills."

Mia laughed and Courtney stood up, gathering up her laptop. "Thanks a lot for the help on the sheets, Mia."

"If you have any more questions, please ask." Mia smiled kindly at her. "And when you're ready to start selling, put me first in line. I'd love to hear the entire presentation, and help you think of any questions that might come up."

"Thanks." Courtney's wan face was happier than when she'd entered the room. "I'll do that." She left with a cheerful wave.

Mia looked at her watch and decisively rose to her feet. Time for her team meeting. She walked briskly down the hall and opened the door to the hospitality team room, smiling encouragingly at the expectant faces. Most of the team from the restaurant was here. Carlos tapped his foot impatiently. Joseph leaned insouciantly against the wall in the back. Red-haired Nick bounced on the edge of his seat, his excitement at being in at a real live murder investigation bubbling over. Kayla, smiling like a hostess, handed the floor to her.

"Everyone here who can take the time?" Mia asked. Nods all around. "Good."

"I want to thank everyone here for keeping the hotel running smoothly despite the," Mia paused, "recent trouble." She beamed benignly around the room and feet shuffled. "I want to make sure everyone understands that if they know anything at all about the explosion or anything relevant about any of the guests involved, they should tell the police. Tell your immediate superior and they will make certain you have time to talk with the police."

"What if we don't really know something?" Nick asked quickly. "Like if we overheard someone talking?"

"If you think it might be relevant to Ms. Hathway's death in any way, you should tell the police. Naturally, anything not relevant to her death should remain private to our guests, as usual." Mia smiled reassuringly. "The police are used to sorting out what is important and what isn't in a case of potential murder." She didn't know that she actually believed that about this particular police chief, but telling the police everything was still the right thing to do. She thoughtfully held Nick's gaze, "If you're nervous about it, you can tell me, and I'll be glad to help you decide what to do next."

She saw Carlos give her a knowing grin, quickly averting his smirk. Of course Mia wanted to buttonhole Nick and find out what he knew. She was doubtful Chief White could solve his way out of a paper bag, from what she'd seen.

Mia continued smoothly, "If anyone else would like some guidance, please ask me or Mr. Curry." He nodded to her from his post in the back of the room, debonair as always, in an appropriately broken-in tweed jacket. "If anyone feels they need a lawyer for a talk with the police, we can arrange guidance with one of the hotel lawyers, free of charge. I know many people are nervous about talking with the police. I want to make sure you're as comfortable as possible, under the circumstances." No one seemed interested in that. Good, she thought. At least no one was worried they'd done anything criminal.

"Now, I know some of you take your own boats to and from the island." She nodded to Carlos. "While under normal circumstances, that's completely fine, I'm a bit concerned about the safety of your boats..."

Andrew Michaud opened both double doors with a resounding crash that bounced them off the wall. He was closely followed by his wife in a bright pink flowered apron. "I knew you'd want to try this!" He made a beeline for Mia with a small plate piled high with golden yellow mushrooms, their delicious aroma wafting through the room.

"Andrew, Tina? What are you doing here?"

He shoved the mushrooms two inches from her face, beaming proudly. "You have to try these."

"Yes, but we're in the middle of a team meeting." Mia inhaled the delicious aroma, surrendering to temptation. "Those do smell wonderful."

Tina said cheerfully, apron straining against her large bust. "He just had to find you to try them. I think it's one of the best recipes we've made."

"Just a soupçon of nutmeg, that was the key!" Andrew's enthusiasm was pervasive.

"Might I have a tiny bite?" asked Carlos. "I've never had chanterelles that fresh before. I can't believe they grow in our woods here." He eyed the plate with interest.

"Of course, of course," Andrew held the plate welcomingly. "You were so kind about letting me use your kitchen." He glanced sidelong at Mia, reddening slightly. "After the lunch preparation was over, of course. And we'll finish before dinner preparations."

"I think we'll adjourn the meeting so you all can get back to work," Mia said. "Thank you so much for coming through for us in a very trying time. I appreciate the work you're doing." She raised her voice, "Anyone who wants to contact the police, wants a lawyer or to talk with me, please just ask."

She delicately took a bite of the proffered mushrooms. "Absolutely delicious. The depth of umami —just amazing." Mia smiled at the Michauds. "Thank you so much for letting me taste them."

Tina beamed, while the room crowded around the plate for a taste. "We wish more people knew what mushrooms tasted like fresh. It makes all the difference in the world to have them the same day they're picked."

"And this well prepared," Carlos told them. "Very

152

well done. You must let Chef Ava taste them."

They glowed at the praise.

"I wonder if it would be possible to do guided food tours here?" Mia asked. "Let people try local foods after seeing them harvested themselves."

"What a wonderful idea!" the Michauds enthused. "We can show you so many foods in just this season."

Joseph tasted his bite of mushroom with a thoughtful expression on his face. "Delicious," was all he said aloud. Mia could see the wheels turning in his head on a new idea for the hotel.

A reinvigorated crowd spilled out of the room, chatting about ideas for foraging menus.

Nick, looking very uncomfortable, held back so he was the last left in the room.

"Hello, Nick," Mia gestured to a nearby chair. "So you have something you overheard, then?"

"It wasn't much," he muttered, carefully not looking at her. "I shouldn't have brought it up here, in front of everyone."

"Nevertheless, you did. So tell me about it and we'll figure it out what to do next together," she said kindly, taking a seat.

Nick fell into the chair opposite her, gangly limbs awkward. "All right." His eyes darted to hers, then skittered away nervously. "Well, I missed the first boat home. I forgot to clean one counter and Chef Carlos sent me back to do it." His eyes flickered. "I kindof forgot for a minute, then tried to do it real quick. But I wasn't fast enough. I ran for the boat." He grinned cheekily at Mia, "Almost made it, but they were pulling away as I came around the corner. So I was stuck for an extra three hours."

"That's too bad," Mia commiserated.

"It happens sometimes. I can always sleep in the crew break room, if I want to." He shrugged easily. "Sometimes we stay overnight if there's a big storm and guests here. They ask for volunteers, and we get overtime pay. I always stay if I can. It's a lot of fun! They still have the old servants' quarters from way back when. It feels like you're sleeping in a haunted house."

"But not actually haunted," Mia reminded him, hoping he wasn't telling guests it was.

"I wish," Nick said fervently. "Anyway, all of the guys stay in the same room, and we tell ghost stories all night. In the morning, we have the best breakfasts ever. Pancakes and bacon and sausage and all the pastries we want. We get these little honey and cream cheese ones from the town bakery that literally melt in your mouth. And there's ham, and waffles," he itemized the list with a dreamy look on his round freckled face.

"But you didn't stay overnight this time," Mia recalled him to the present day.

"No, not this time," he agreed with heartfelt disappointment. "That's only when it storms bad and it's not safe to take the boat. This time, I missed the boat, so I was just waiting around for the next one. Anyway, I know I wasn't supposed to go in the guest areas unless I'm working, but it was the middle of the

154

night and," he sneaked a glance at Mia, "well, I did. I love the library. It's like being in a castle."

Mia nodded, carefully keeping her face expressionless. Now was not the time for reprimands.

"So I was lying on the sofa there, looking up at that awesome ceiling, and some guests came in." His eyes twitched in her direction, then back at the floor. "So I couldn't get out without them seeing me, you know, and I wasn't supposed to be there, so I hid behind that big chair in the corner." He looked at her for reassurance.

"Go on," Mia told him.

"Well, they were arguing, big time. She yelled at him, what about my money? And he said she'd get it like she'd been promised." He wrinkled his nose. "She didn't seem to believe she'd get it."

"Who were they?"

"I don't know. I mean, I know the man was that Paul Baker. I saw him. You know, the one who said he was going to marry the woman who died. I saw him."

"And the woman?"

"I don't know. I mean, I guess it was the woman who died, but I never saw her. And I never heard the woman who died's voice."

"But you recognized the man?"

"Yeah, he wasn't all screechy like she was. He just had his normal voice, which I'd heard. She was yelling, but kind of whispering too, trying not to be overheard. All high pitched and angry. I mean, I guess it was his girlfriend." He shook his head in disgust. "Sounded like a girlfriend, anyway."

"It's too bad you couldn't tell who it was for sure," Mia said with disappointment. "Did you hear anything else?"

"Not really. It just sounded like he owed her money or promised her money or something. He kept saying she'd get her money, and she kept asking how could he get it now, she controls everything. I guess she meant his wife. He told the woman yelling at him, calm down, relax, I have a plan, she'd get her money. They walked off after that, and I got out of the library quick." Nick looked relieved to have that off his chest.

Mia nodded thoughtfully, "Well, Nick, it could have been Melissa Hathway speaking to Paul Baker. It was definitely Paul Baker, so you do need to tell the police about it."

His face fell. "Right now? My mom's at work."

"I think tomorrow will be soon enough." Mia looked at him, "You're how old? Eighteen?" She was sure he was younger.

"No, ma'am, I'm seventeen. This is my summer job," Nick said proudly. "I started last year."

"I see. Well, you need to talk with your parents about what they want you to do, but I think, since you're underage, you need a lawyer with you when you talk to the police."

His face fell, "My mom can't afford a lawyer. I mean, I'm doing this to pay for school."

Mia quickly reassured him, "There's no reason for you to pay for a lawyer, Nick. You're one of the our hospitality team and I offered free legal advice to everyone who felt like they needed it." She smiled ruefully, "I've met Chief White. I feel more comfortable having my team members represented by a lawyer, especially for someone under eighteen."

"Yeah, the chief hates my guts," Nick confided.

"And why would that be?" Mia asked him, grinning at him.

"Well, I might have played truant from school some, and he caught me a few times," Nick grinned at her, freckled cheeks rounded. "It's been a while, but he's not the forgetting type."

"I see," Mia grinned back. "Well, Mr. Curry or I can accompany you to talk with the police, your mother can go with you, or you can get a lawyer, paid for by the hotel. Whatever you and your mother decide is fine, but the police do need to know everything that happened that night as soon as possible."

"Mr. Curry is going to go ballistic when he finds out I was in the library without a reason."

"This time, he has bigger things on his mind. I wouldn't try it a second time, though," Mia warned with a smile.

"Not likely," Nick said with a look of relief. "I like my job."

"Is there anything else worrying you?" Mia asked.

"No, that was it. Thanks, Ms. Mia. I'll ask my mom tonight who I should take with me to the police and talk to them tomorrow."

"Don't put it off any longer than that," Mia told him. She knew teenage boys would put unpleasant things off as long as they could. They'd plan to do them, just later. And later didn't usually turn up. "You need to tell them first thing tomorrow what you heard, otherwise it looks like you're hiding something. That would be much worse. We don't want the Chief getting any ideas about you."

Nick looked nervous again and nodded, "Tomorrow. Yes, ma'am." He saluted and left the room, glad to be done answering questions for today.

7

Blue Sea

L auren adjusted the tiller and gazed out at the distant horizon. "What a gorgeous morning." The waves slapped gently on the sides of the boat, and the salt air filled her lungs.

"It's going to be a perfect day, isn't it?" Max hauled in the main sheet a little.

"It is." Lauren smiled at the sea. "I feel pretty guilty for skipping out of the hotel to go sailing."

"Oh, it's not your fault," Max told her, his eyes crinkling into tiny laugh lines. He propped his legs comfortably up, wedging his body into place in the small cockpit. "I kidnapped you."

"You did kidnap me." Lauren laughed. "You were right, though, I needed to get away for a bit."

Max looked out at the horizon, hand tight on the line. "Beautiful little boat, this." They had taken out the Herreshoff twelve and a half they had both coveted a sail in.

"Yes, she sails like a dream." Lauren looked back at the distant hotel. "Remember sailing when we were kids? You'd talk me into a quick sail, and we'd be gone all day in that little boat you had."

"I loved that old boat," Max sighed. "I practically built her." He leaned back, trimming the sail slightly.

"And rebuilt her from scraps every winter. That shed was wicked cold." Lauren shivered at the memory of Max and her working on dark winter nights, getting the scrap heap of a sailboat ready to sail the next summer. And now they were sailing this beauty, even if it was just a loan. Maybe, next summer, she'd get a little sailboat, and they'd go sailing again. She met Max's eyes, calmly reading her thoughts with a small smile on his face.

She shook herself. Today's plans were all she could handle. "Look, I'm sorry, but we do need to go back soon. I don't want the police to think I'm skipping out. Chief White hates me as it is. He'd love to track me down as a fugitive. And Uncle Harvey is coming sometime today or tomorrow. More paperwork." She rolled her eyes.

"He said this afternoon, right?"

"He said maybe today. He was still working on some details about the trust transfer. I know I'll see him tomorrow for that, on my birthday. Plus, I need to file for divorce before we break the trust. I might have to get divorced first; I don't know. I do know Paul's not getting my family business. Pop would come back just to haunt me." Lauren sighed, losing her smile. "I can't

believe someone killed Melissa. Actually killed her."
The boat changed course slightly as her hand shook on
the tiller.

Max's eyes narrowed in thought. "I really have no
idea who would do something like that. Do you?"

"I know I'm the obvious suspect," Lauren put in.
"But I just didn't care enough about her to kill her. It
was Paul I was really mad at."

"She still wasn't exactly your favorite person,"
Max said with a wry smile. He added quickly, "Not
that you'd kill her. She wasn't my favorite either."

"No." Lauren smoothed her dark hair into its
clip. "But, in a way, she was my out of the marriage. I
hadn't been happy with Paul for a long time." She
laughed shortly. "Our marriage was obviously a huge
mistake I was stuck living in. I was mad at finding
them together—it was pretty awful just seeing them
like that, but—" She fiddled with the tiller. "If it hadn't
been Melissa, it probably would have been someone
else. I know that."

"I'm sorry," Max's eyes met hers, then flickered
away. "Been there too." His mouth tightened, lines
deepening.

"Yeah, I know," Lauren said sympathetically.
"Well, you can tell me how to get through a divorce
then."

He barked a laugh. "I up and left when I found
out she was seeing someone on the side. Got the
lawyers to handle the divorce. I just wanted out."

"Sound plan." Lauren sighed. "I was planning to
hand it over to Uncle Harvey."

161

"He'll make sure Paul doesn't get anything. He never liked Paul much." Max squinted out at the horizon, sun lines around his eyes deepening.

"How do you know?" Lauren asked curiously.

"Just a guess," Max was quietly noncommittal.

Lauren's face turned beet red. "You haven't been discussing me, have you?"

"No, Lauren," Max said tolerantly, looking at her. "We haven't been discussing you. I've just heard him talking with Paul, that's all. He was," he searched for the right words, "politely antagonistic."

"Oh," Lauren's smile was a little teary. "I'm sorry."

"Hey, it's okay." Max let out the main sail, adjusting the jib at the same time with an easy hand. "Harvey did ask me who I thought killed Melissa."

"What'd you say?"

"I said I didn't know." He looked directly at her eyes sharply. "And that's the truth, Lauren. I'm so damn frustrated because I feel like I should know. I've worked at Tisserande for a year. I know all the people involved. Heck, I grew up with most of them. The answer should be obvious. And I just don't know who the murderer is. I don't even know who could murder someone, besides Paul, and he didn't have any reason to kill Melissa."

Lauren's voice was quietly controlled. "Do you think someone was trying to kill me?"

Max darted a glance at her, "Maybe." He scanned the horizon. "Seems more likely than Melissa."

"Why?" Lauren's voice was tightly disciplined,

but her hand shook on the tiller. The boat wobbled and she readjusted her course.

"You're rich, Lauren." He made the simple statement of fact. "Lots of people weren't happy about you moving the factory back to Maine. They thought it'd ruin the company, and they'd lose their jobs."

"Lots of people were happy."

"Sure. I know I am." Max smiled at her, eyes crinkling. "I'm thrilled about it and not just because I get new machines to play with."

"Yeah, right," Lauren teased. "You were totally bored with the distribution equipment."

"I had a good boss, though." He grinned at her again. "But pretty much your entire management was against it."

"Jeremy wasn't."

"Well, no, Jeremy would love whatever insane ideas you came up with," Max smiled. "You could paint the building pink, and he'd cheer you on."

Lauren protested, "He's very good at marketing."

"He works hard at whatever tasks you give him," Max said, smoothly noncommittal. "Jeremy's good people and he's family."

They sailed in silence for a minute, wind blowing so they barely skimmed the water. The only sound was the soft slapping of the waves on the boat, flying along the blue water.

Max broke the moment. "Paul and Cynthia weren't happy about you building the factory," he said bluntly. "They're both here."

Lauren looked into the undulating water, sun

163

glinting in intricate dancing patterns. The boat rocked slightly in the breeze, waves slapping the sides. They were in deep water here. "No, they were both against it."

"Money?" Max asked.

"Yeah, it'd mean a lot less profits for a few years. Less in their bonus checks, which are tied to profits. I thought it was a good trade off for the health of our town. They didn't." Lauren's voice was heavy. "But it's my company."

"So you overrode them," Max said thoughtfully. "Paul knew he wouldn't get the company if you died?" he questioned, looking out at the horizon to avoid Lauren's eyes.

"He knew that," she said shortly. "He'd get some money if I died, but not much. Most of my capital is tied up in Tisserande. If I died today, with no kids, the company would be distributed to the employees under my parents' trust. Jeremy would get more shares than Paul, since he's in my parents' will."

"But you weren't firing Paul or Cynthia?" Max questioned.

Lauren fiddled with her hair clip. "I wasn't firing them, exactly. But I was planning on Paul, especially, having a lot less control over the company as we moved back home. He chose to move most of them overseas in the first place, you know. I never liked that, but I didn't have much say in it, back then. So I went along with it." She ran her hand along the smooth wood of the boat.

"So he wasn't happy, but he wouldn't get that

much money if you died suddenly," Max summed up. "So he wouldn't actually benefit from your death?"

"Yeah, he'll probably get more actual cash from a divorce settlement and severance package," Lauren said bitterly.

"And Cynthia's job would be about the same with the new factory? Except for bonuses, of course."

"Yes, finance is finance. It doesn't really matter where the money comes from or goes to, spreadsheets are the same. Though it sounds like Paul told her to lie to me with them." Lauren added, "I should get her product profitability breakdown today. I should probably be more concerned about that, but I'm so spleeny about the murder I don't have anything left over."

"Yeah, I know." Max shook his head. "Maybe it was one of the sales team. They all hated Melissa's guts."

"I got that from the meeting. I wish someone had told me," Lauren tightened her lips.

"I doubt Paul would have let you do anything about it," Max commented dryly. "But the sales team are my primary suspects."

"I can't imagine Jake and Blake killing anyone," Lauren laughed. "They don't care enough about anything to bother."

"Their sales are actually pretty good, from what they let drop," Max replied. "I think you might be surprised. Jeremy speaks highly of them, and he runs a pretty tight ship. If Melissa had been stealing their best sales out from under them, they might be angrier than they let on."

The jib luffed a bit. Lauren changed tack slightly, and Max let out the jib line. He speculated, "So you think it's Courtney?"

Lauren said sharply, "No, I don't think it's Courtney." She looked out at the horizon. "I like Courtney. She's really sweet and her mom is the best."

"Uh huh," Max agreed.

"And Jeremy likes her, I think."

"Does he now?"

"Jeremy's been really lonely. Lately, he's been going to lunch with her, dropping by to help with her mom." Lauren rolled her eyes, "You know how it takes Jeremy forever to ask a girl out."

"So you don't want it to be Courtney? Or you think it's Courtney and feel bad about that?"

She prevaricated. "I don't really think it's her. Just, well, she really seemed to hate Melissa at that meeting. It sounds like Melissa had stolen a lot of sales from Courtney. With her mom so sick, she can't easily move. That has to be frustrating, not to be able to do anything about it. I wish she'd told me." Lauren sighed reluctantly, then admitted, "And I saw her on the dock that morning."

Max pounced, "What?"

"It wasn't a big deal," Lauren told him. "She was just looking at the water when I ran down to get my bag. She wasn't anywhere near the Harrier."

"Did you tell her Melissa was taking the boat?" Max asked sharply.

Lauren said hesitantly, "Well, yes. I did. But I'm

sure she wouldn't have done anything to it."

"It would just take a minute to splash some fuel around, disable the bilge blower." Max's voice was grim. "Did you tell the police?"

"Well, no," Lauren said. She excused herself, saying, "Uncle Harvey told me to not volunteer anything. And the police chief didn't ask me."

"Well, that was numb, Lauren," Max sighed. "Now if you say you saw her there, the police will say you're making it up."

Lauren's eyes went wide, and the tiller wobbled the boat. "I didn't think of that."

"Obviously not," Max jerked on the jib, then let the wind fill it. "So, much as we like Courtney, she's our obvious suspect."

"Her mom needs her."

"And lots of people need you. You or Courtney in jail, I know which I'd pick."

"There has to be someone else," Lauren wailed. "There just has to be. I like Courtney. And I really think Jeremy might be interested in her. You know how he's been since Deborah moved."

"There aren't that many people at the hotel," Max refused to be distracted. "It has to be one of them."

"Maybe it was someone Melissa knew before she came to Maine. Someone staying at the hotel. We wouldn't know who else she knew."

"Maybe," Max said grudgingly. "She's been here, what, two years? That's a long time to wait to kill someone."

"Yeah." Lauren flailed, "Maybe it was just some psycho killer who didn't know her at all? Maybe kids messing around and not realizing what would happen? Or just an accident, something wrong with the engine?"

"Tell you the truth, I don't know how they'll prove it wasn't an accident," Max said. "It sank wicked deep, roundabout there." He pointed. "I don't see them diving for it." He looked into the dark blue water, considering. "I don't see how they could possibly prove it was murder even if they pulled it back up. There wasn't much left to find anyway." He shuddered once, hard, and the jib strained in its cleat.

"Could it have been an accident, after all? Just a horrible accident?" Lauren asked fervently.

"No, I don't see how it could have been. It was murder, right enough. But if I was accused of murder, I'd sure say it was an accident. Hard to prove otherwise." He looked hard at Lauren. "If you're accused, that's your story. Could have been her not running the bilge blower and a fuel leak. Don't suggest anything concrete, though, or they'll use that to accuse you. Let Harvey do any suggesting. Impossible to prove murder, really. Stick to that, don't suggest anything at all, and they will never be able to prove otherwise."

"The police chief hates me. Paul fired his aunt when the factory closed, and he's still mad about it." Lauren shivered in the bright sunlight. "He's sure I killed her. So are Mandy and John. They're awful."

"Just stick to the it must have been a terrible boat

accident story. Quit talking about murder. He can't prove a thing," Max advised as they sailed up to the Moose Isle Inn dock and dropped the sails, working together to fold them with the ease of long practice.

Lauren shook her head, "That's not what happened, is it?" Her voice was quiet and scared.

"No, it wasn't. Stick near people, Lauren. Me or Jeremy. I wouldn't trust anyone else, especially not Mandy or John. We still don't know what happened, whether you or Melissa was the target."

Lauren shivered again, goosebumps in the summer sun. Max gave her a hand up onto the dock and tied off. The harbor master came hurrying up to check potential damage to his precious boat.

"Hey, Douglas," Max smiled at him. "Thanks for the boat loan. She's a beauty."

"Ayuh," Douglas grunted. "Looks like you got her back alright."

"Not like the Harrier," Max added with distinct sadness.

"No, it's a wicked shame, that was. She was a right fine boat." Douglas ran his eyes along his diminished fleet. The boats ran the gamut from rough and ready boats the team might haul supplies in, to sleek wooden runabouts with gleaming wood and the grande dame Hinckley Picnic Boat. It was an impressive collection, both new and old. All were in gleaming, pristine condition.

"Will you be getting another to replace her?" Lauren asked.

"Up to the boss," Douglas grunted. "That

husband of yours had better not come trying to rent any boats, though. You tell him that."

"Paul was trying to rent a boat? When?"

"Think he wanted to go after you two," Douglas muttered, staring at the dock. "I told him no boats for rent right now."

"Thanks, Douglas," Lauren smiled in thanks.

"Ayuh," Douglas grunted.

They headed back to the hotel.

Andrew and Tina Michaud stepped mincingly onto the dock, bouncing it like a trampoline. His arms were entangled in a fishing pole, filament wound in great loops around him. She carried an oversize wicker picnic basket with a red checkered tablecloth coyly peeping out.

"Hi, we wanted to rent a boat to go fishing?" Andrew asked. He pulled his arms out of the fishing pole web and swung it around, narrowly missing Douglas's eyes.

Douglas, completely expressionless, moved deftly out of the way. "What kind of boat?"

"A fishing boat?" Andrew considered, looking at the bobbing boats.

"A sailboat or a motorboat?" Douglas asked warily.

"Is there one with one of those cute little grills on the back?" Tina asked, patting her wicker basket, smiling maternally.

"Oh, I don't think a sailboat. They look complicated. I think a motorboat. That would be just like driving a car, right? They've got a steering wheel, gas and brakes. Nothing to it." Andrew grinned with his decision, swung the fishing pole again and Douglas ducked under it with a grunt. "We'll take a motor boat."

Douglas looked lovingly at his sleek collection of boats and back at the enthusiastic couple. "No boats available right now."

"Oh," Andrew said, his pole sagging. "None at all?"

"None," said Douglas firmly. "You want to take one of the lobster tours out of the town harbor."

"They have fishing?" Andrew perked up and his pole whipped around. Douglas ducked automatically.

"Ayuh. You'll catch fish on those. Just go to town and ask for the tour boats." Douglas walked away before they could ask another question.

Jake and Blake spilled into the interview room, jostling for space in the doorway.

Chief White grimaced at their antics, "Siddown."

They abruptly sat. Jake instantly began a monologue. "Are you sure Melissa's death was murder? It might have been an accident. Accidents happen all the time around boats. I remember my uncle was working on his engine. It wasn't a boat engine, it was his truck, but an engine anyway. It caught fire when he was leaning over. He didn't have eyebrows for a year after that. Drew them on with his wife's eyebrow pencil. You wouldn't believe how silly he looked. We laughed and laughed." He looked expectantly at the chief. "And my cousin, Carl, he was working on a generator when he—" Jake trailed off as Chief White's glare apparently bored into his skull.

"We're here to discuss Melissa Hathway, not your relatives." He glared forbiddingly at the two.

"Yes, sir," they chorused.

He continued, growling the words, "Did you know Ms. Hathway was having an affair with Paul Taylor?"

Jake offered, "I found them in the break room once. Pretty obvious what they were doing." He laughed nervously.

Blake sniggered.

"Do you think it's funny a woman is dead?" the chief thundered.

"No, no, of course not," Jake assured him. Blake simply shook his head no.

"Do you know of anyone other than Mrs. Baker who wanted to kill Ms. Hathway?"

Jake answered quickly, "No, I don't think anyone else wanted Melissa dead." Realizing what he'd said, "Wait a sec, I don't think Lauren wanted Melissa dead."

"Lauren would just fire her," Blake put in, uncrossing his legs and leaning forward. "Why would she kill Melissa?"

"Ms. Hathway was having an affair with her

husband," the chief stated. "I doubt Mrs. Baker felt friendly towards her."

Jake blurted, "Yeah, but not liking her and killing her. I mean, that's two totally different things."

"Once Lauren got over the shock, she'd probably thank the woman for taking Paul off her hands," Blake added. "She was going to see her lawyer for a divorce anyway. Paul's an asshole."

"Huh," the chief grunted in clear disbelief. He aligned his pencil precisely with his notebook. "Other than pure speculation, can you think of anyone else who would want Melissa Hathway dead?"

They looked at each other, clearly torn about who to toss to the wolves. Jake demurred, "Why would it be one of us? It could be some old boyfriend of Melissa's or something."

"Do you know of any such boyfriends?" The chief was clearly not buying it.

"No," Jake said uncertainly. "But she must have had some. I mean, she always came back from trips with a lot of new stuff. Jewelry and clothes, you know. Of course, she really liked to shop," he trailed off. "I didn't really know her that well. We didn't do sales calls together or anything."

Jake and Blake glanced at each other again in quick communication, then shrugged identically. "We didn't know her that well," Jake finished.

"Let me know if you think of anything relevant," the chief ordered. "You may go."

They fought to be the first out of the interview room.

Harvey Thompson was having a very long day. Against his better judgement, he had asked all three of Lauren's other trustees to meet at his office. Mandy Martin had shown up half an hour early, as usual. Her honey sweet voice grated, as she explained in detail her plan to confine Lauren in a mental hospital, for her own good. "It will be so much better to keep her from running Tisserande Linens into bankruptcy. Paul tells me she is planning on completely destroying the company for no reason whatsoever. It has to be a psychological problem. I was watching this talk show the other day that had pathological liars on it. You wouldn't believe the things they did to the people that trusted them. And they just couldn't help themselves." She looked at him with simmering hatred. "Lauren is just like those poor creatures."

Harvey sighed. He intensely disliked this acid woman in her candy pink dress. He couldn't wait until he no longer had to attend trustee meeting with her. "Mandy, Lauren is not insane. We can't lock her up for no reason."

"Why else would she kill an innocent woman?" she laid down the law. "She must be crazy. We're her trustees. We have a clear duty to help her and preserve Tisserande Linens." Her tightly plastic skin stretched over a smug sneer. "It's for her own good."

Harvey chose his words carefully. "I will repeat, Lauren did not kill Melissa Hathway."

"Paul says she did," she rejoined, patting her stiff artificially blond hair. "I think he would know if his wife murdered someone."

"Paul was having an affair with Ms. Hathway," he continued pedantically.

"He was not!" Mandy smirked knowingly, smoothing her shiny skirt over pudgy thighs with a secretive smile. "Paul would never do such a thing. He and Lauren might be going through a little," she smiled to herself, "difficulty, but he'd never take up with that little tramp."

Harvey wondered briefly exactly how Paul had gotten his job as the CEO of Tisserande Linens. He'd tried his best not to hire Paul at the time, but had been overruled.

"He was caught," he coughed delicately, "in flagrante delicto with Ms. Hathway."

"Lauren must be lying," smirked Mandy. "Paul would never do a thing like that. I heard him saying he wouldn't take Lauren back. Lauren's probably the one having an affair, not Paul."

"There were two other witnesses to the incident besides Lauren. Lauren's cousin, Jeremy Taylor, and the hotel owner. From what I understand, the affair was quite embarrassingly public."

"That's impossible. They must be lying. Paul would never—" Mandy Martin's face had gone white under her beach tan makeup. Pink rouge showed in bright blotches.

"Paul admitted it," Harvey stated. "He told the police he was going to marry Ms. Hathway."

"He told me it was a dirty lie," she rejoined. "Why would he possibly say that?"

"Since he stated otherwise on several public occasions, I have no idea why he would tell you that. He was quite public about his affair with Ms. Hathway after it was discovered." Harvey went on before she could cut him off. "Lauren, as was proper, informed him at the time she would be divorcing him and made an appointment with me the next morning."

"And then she killed that woman," Mandy primped her hair again, refusing to give up.

"Lauren did not kill Melissa Hathway."

Mandy just sniffed.

Harvey continued, "As her lawyer, I will of course trace any slanders of my client to their source and prosecute them fully."

Her smooth face melted into a plastic stillness.

"As her trustee, naturally you will support me in this." He smiled grimly. "We certainly don't want any false rumors spread that might hurt her or the company."

Mandy Martin made an inarticulate sound. Harvey took that to mean agreement—or at least quiet. She fiddled with her dress, her purse and redid her gooey pink lipstick, avoiding his glare. Harvey looked through his paperwork one more time in the awkward silence, trying to ignore her frequent sighs.

It was a welcome relief when the other two trustees arrived. A tall straight backed man, Tom

Saunders, had served with Lauren's father in the navy. He had continued his service until a recent retirement, unlike Jules Tisserande, who had returned home after his brief navy stint to run the family business. Tom shook Harvey's hand firmly and sat at the conference table, placing an empty notepad and pen at his seat.

John Libby, face pink and bloated, immediately started talking, "So poor Lauren is insane? Poor girl, poor girl. What can we do to help her?" He shook his head sadly, resting his pudgy hands on his protruding belly. "Mandy says we need to lock her up where she can't cause any more deaths. It's probably for the best. For the best." John's father had been friends with Jules's father. Harvey saw no other reason he'd been named Lauren's trustee. The Tisserandes, like everyone else, had not expected to die so young, leaving a too young Lauren in the hands of her trustees.

"Lauren insane? Don't believe that. Seemed fine last time I saw her," Tom Saunders stated. He leaned forward intently. "Any evidence she killed this woman? Doesn't seem like her. She's a sensible girl."

"Who else is there, Tom, dear?" Mandy's tone was cloyingly sweet. "The poor girl is insane. I understand she's been failing for some time. Look what she's done about spending all that money on a factory in that decrepit little town." She smiled archly at him, "Absolutely everyone knows you have to go overseas to make any money now."

Tom broke in, "Hold on a minute, Mandy." He tapped his pen, "I talked with Lauren about this one a few weeks ago and I think she's right. Machinery's

177

changed a lot in the last decade, and Megeso Point's been suffering without the factory. It's her hometown. I think she's making the right moral decision and not a half bad financial one."

"Tom, Tom," Mandy smiled sweetly. "You big strong naval men don't know anything about business any more than little Lauren. You can't run a business with morals." She snickered.

Tom Saunders's eyes narrowed, "Excuse me, Mandy?"

"You just don't have any business experience, like I do. So manly and unworldly." She buffed her nails on her dress and arched her back proudly.

"I think I can read a spreadsheet better than someone who's spent her life marrying money and doing a piss poor job of it too," Tom burst out. "The only reason you're a trustee at all is you were Lauren's mother's second cousin. Not your so called business experience. As far as I can tell, your trustee income is about all you have going for you right now. And that ends tomorrow, unless you find a way to stretch it out. Guess you wouldn't mind sending poor little Lauren to the loony bin if you get to keep the checks rolling in." His nose wrinkled in disgust.

Mandy's face reddened as she struggled with her voice. "Well, I'll..."

Harvey hurriedly stepped in, clearing his throat precisely. "We're all in this together, people. Let's remember our responsibility," he glared at Mandy, "is Lauren's well being."

John said, "Of course, of course. Poor girl, poor

girl," he added, making sure everyone understood he felt sorry for Lauren.

Harvey pushed his glasses up his nose."I want to make one thing completely clear to everyone present." He coughed for emphasis. "Lauren has not been accused of murder."

"Just a matter of time," John muttered.

Harvey ignored him, "Lauren is not insane. She is not a murderer."

"Yeah, right," Mandy mocked sweetly.

"I feel certain Lauren will be cleared of any wrongdoing, and the real culprit will be found shortly," he stated with a lot more certainty about the police doing their job than he felt. He knew Chief White from previous cases. Harvey cleared his throat again. "I've called you here for another reason entirely."

John asked, "What else could possibly be as important as murder?" His small eyes peered out from piggy folds at the other trustees. "I really feel we should get Lauren committed as quickly as possible. To protect her, of course. Certainly before the trust is dissolved."

Mandy agreed, saccharine sweet, "It's in her best interest." She opened her eyes wide for emphasis, but her face stayed in its plastic mold.

Harvey slapped his hand down on the table for emphasis in a move completely unlike him. "Listen to me. I was going over the final accounting notes for Tisserande Linens before we removed the company from trusteeship this week. Money is missing from the company accounts. A lot of money."

Mandy's mouth fell open in a wide oh. Harvey wondered if it would crack in the unaccustomed shape.

"It can't be," John stated dogmatically. "We check the accounting every year. Mandy and I spent an entire day last year going over it with Paul and Cynthia. We had dinner at that Italian restaurant on Main Street." His pudgy hands clenched and unclenched in a sudden spasm.

Tom said nothing, leaning forward intently.

"I had the company's financial data audited by an independent accountant in preparation for the management changeover." Harvey shoved his glasses up and peered at his audience for their reaction. "The last independent audit occurred almost two years ago. No independent audit has been done since."

"How much is missing?" Tom asked bluntly.

"About fifteen million dollars," Harvey stated decisively.

The room went dead quiet, finally broken by John saying uncertainly, "That can't be right."

"It can't be," Mandy accused wildly. "I bet Lauren's hidden it somewhere. Offshore accounts or something."

Harvey looked hard at her. "You do realize Lauren does not have access to company funds currently? She draws a paycheck twice a month, just like everyone else."

Mandy's lips compressed. "That's not proof. Of course she took it. Who else would?"

Tom stepped in, "Why would she? Lauren couldn't have taken it. Who has direct access to the accounts?"

"We do, as Lauren's trustees and board. We are responsible for that missing money." He looked around the room. He saw John visibly deflate in his chair. Mandy's face twisted into an ugly sneer. Tom had stiffened into parade ground posture, face turned hard as teak.

Mandy accused, "Those accountants must be lying. We did that audit two years ago. Everything was fine then."

Harvey steepled his fingers, "I will, of course, be calling for a second independent audit by a different company in a case of this magnitude. However, I doubt the accountants are lying. They have no reason to do so."

"Who else has access?" Tom barked.

Harvey stated shortly, "Paul Baker, as CEO, and Cynthia Clark, as the VP of finance, both have access to the company money. As trustees, we also have access."

"Anyone else?" Tom demanded.

"No official access." He looked around at the room. "Of course, theft is usually not official."

Tom said slowly, "The dead woman was a saleswoman? Could her death be related to the theft?" He tapped one finger on his leg, slowly considering. "That's a lot of missing money."

"I don't know," Harvey said uncertainly. "The accountants are still working on discovery."

Tom subsided slightly, "When will they know? Can they find the money?"

"I have no idea. They say it's a complicated case." Harvey looked at his audience. "And, of course, it's not simply about the money, but the criminal prosecution case."

"Criminal prosecution?" Mandy squeaked. Her bubble gum pink high heeled shoe jogged in place.

"Of course," Harvey said smoothly. "We will not," he looked firmly at Mandy, "let millions be stolen from Lauren without doing our best to recover it, and prosecuting to the full extent of the law."

"Good," Tom stood with decision. "You'll let us know when you have more information?" It was a military order.

Harvey said, "As soon as I can."

"A little late for that, isn't it?" Mandy added. "With fifteen million supposedly gone."

"We'll do our best to find it, since we, as trustees, are responsible. We have, of course, frozen all accounts so no more large transfers can take place."

Mandy muttered bitterly, "It was still probably Lauren." She teetered on her heels as she stood up, then recovered her balance. She left the room without saying goodbye. She was trailed by John Libby, like a pink balloon on a string.

Tom nodded, "Tell Lauren if she needs anything, anything at all, to let me know." He shook his head, "I hate this happened on my watch."

"On all of our watches," Harvey agreed.

Cynthia rapped on Courtney's door, "Courtney, are you in? I wanted to discuss the sales plans with you." Her foot tapped impatiently.

After a few beats, Courtney opened the door into a dark room, looking exhausted, like she hadn't slept last night. "Cynthia, this isn't a great time." The dark circles under her eyes gave witness to that. Her skin looked stretched in pain.

"It'll just take a few minutes," Cynthia urged. "We really need to discuss your upcoming sales plans." She held up her laptop bag.

Courtney reluctantly opened the door to let her in, flipping the lights on. "I'm not done with my sales plan yet," she told her. "I'm working on it, but I'm nowhere near done. It's a completely different market I need to reach, in a lot of cases, so it takes research. I'm not even sure who my potential buyers are yet."

"I know, I know," Cynthia commiserated in tight tones. "I can't believe Lauren is shaking things up like this. We had a good business going, and she's just wrecking it to pieces."

"I don't know," Courtney demurred. "It's a lot of work, but—"

"Our high end lines, made overseas, are much more cost effective than building a whole factory here. Building projects are expensive. That will eat away any profits. Better to keep our current sources."

Courtney agreed with hesitation, "I guess so. But they're not nearly as nice as the new samples," she added, with a wry smile.

"Nothing ever turns out like initial samples," Cynthia informed her glibly. "You know that. It's a lot of money spent for no reason that I can see. It's Lauren's company, though. At least for now," she added with a twitch of her lips.

Courtney said nothing, sitting behind her laptop and rubbing her temples.

"But that's not what I came to discuss with you." Cynthia plumped the cushion behind her back, clearly prepared to stay for a long haul. "Which of our current customers do you think will order the new lines? I want to give her a good future projection. After all, sales brings in the money, so everything is based off of that." She fiddled with her orange framed glasses and crossed her thin legs. "Maybe we can convince her to halt the project if I have the right numbers."

Courtney sighed. "I was trying to put together some historical sales numbers, so I could come up with a solid sales forecast for the new line."

"I know, I know," Cynthia stood and paced restlessly. Her unfortunately formfitting pants highlighted her scraggy legs, as well as her broad beamed posterior. "We want it to look good so no one accuses us of anything." She went into the bathroom, touching up her bright orange lipstick in the mirror. Putting it in her pocket as she came out, she said, "Look, whatever Paul has done to the company is going to look really bad for us, if our numbers don't mesh. We need to be on the same page."

Courtney, with dismay, noticed Cynthia's laptop remained open, so she wasn't leaving any time soon. "Why would they accuse us of anything? They'd have to have some evidence."

"With Paul wanting to cherry-pick sales numbers all the time, it's difficult to show Lauren where we really are financially," Cynthia tapped her nail on a table with a sharp impatient click. "Such a hassle."

"All I know about the numbers is what I've turned in to you and Paul," Courtney said. "I don't know anything else."

"Of course not," Cynthia agreed smoothly. "But I really need to get some idea of future numbers while there's still time to convince Lauren she's making a huge mistake."

"I don't think you're going to be able to talk her out of it." Courtney brushed her hair back and rubbed her temples. "I think it's about more than money with Lauren."

"Nonsense. Everything always comes down to money," Cynthia stated. She pursed her bright lips and tapped her glasses with an orange nail, looking concerned. "Courtney, think for a moment about how this looks to everyone. We don't want anyone to get the idea you're making excuses to not come up with real numbers on this. You don't want to look bad, do you?"

"What?" Courtney straightened up in her chair, frowning.

Cynthia's eyes narrowed. "Simple sales projections don't usually take as long as you're taking. All the fuss about headaches and such. Are you trying to hide something?"

"Trying to hide?" Courtney moved her laptop to the coffee table, standing up. "What do you mean?"

"Everyone knows you went on most of Melissa's sales trips with her."

"So?"

"Maybe you had some sort of side deal going with Melissa."

"I didn't," Courtney said in a whisper. She cleared her throat and spoke firmly. "I didn't have any deal going with Melissa. I barely talked to her."

"Well, you'd say so now, wouldn't you?" Cynthia shrugged. "Why would you still be at Tisserande if you weren't getting something under the table for your trouble? You're too good a saleswoman to not level up."

"My mom," Courtney began, her brown eyes widening.

"Like your mom couldn't live with you somewhere else," Cynthia scoffed. She shrugged. "Look, I don't care what your deal with Melissa was. I'm glad to get rid of that little tart. Any evidence as to who finally did it is at the bottom of the sea, so it's not my concern."

"I didn't kill Melissa," Courtney said harshly.

"Of course not," Cynthia told her, enunciating clearly, as if to a child. "So we need to come up with the right sales numbers, like I said. It'll look better to everyone." She stared Courtney down until the younger woman folded into her chair and reached for her laptop. "We're going to be here awhile."

Mia leaned back into the soft cushions of her spa chair, waiting for her treatment. Soft murmurs of relaxation and peaceful music filled the long room. The air wafted the subtle scent of sweet beach roses, mixed with the sharp tang of the sea, and tiny candles echoed the aroma with their golden flames. A rough hewn pink granite waterfall wall splashed gently; water trickling down in the atmosphere of utter repose.

"Hello, Ms. Mia," a cheerfully round woman draped in a soft gray wrap greeted her. "I wondered when I'd see you this trip. How have you been?"

"Hi, Janice, I'm good. How are the kids?"

"My oldest just graduated high school. Can you believe it?" Janice smiled widely.

"Time really flies, doesn't it? What is she doing next?"

"An engineering degree, with a full scholarship, thank goodness." Janice smiled in maternal pride.

"Good for Danielle," Mia said. "And Tony?"

"Doing well at school, but you know boys. You have to keep your eye on them all the time. He's got a summer job mowing lawns now. I think it'll keep him too busy for trouble. He didn't want to work at the hotel along with his mom."

Mia laughed, remembering some of the trouble her boys had got in to. "Mine were always much better when they had summer jobs. Busy is good." A few months of long hours bussing tables or working on the cleaning crew at their Atlanta hotel, made her kids relieved to return to school. "Less time to get into trouble."

"You'd better believe it," Janice told her. "So just a manicure today? No treatments?"

"This trip is pretty busy for me so far, but I'll be back again soon for the full spa treatment." She held out her hands with their slightly chipped manicure. "This is just a quick maintenance visit."

Janice examined her hands with professional care. "It looks like you've been climbing trees," she said with a laugh.

"Maybe a few rocks," Mia guiltily admitted. "I can't resist seeing what's around the next corner."

Janice chuckled, "You and your walks. You'll get yourself into trouble someday."

"Maine is made for long walks." Mia settled back in her chair as Janice took charge of her nails.

"Yours aren't the worst I've seen today. Yesterday, a woman came in with her hands all scraped up from falling on the beach. Completely raw, looked like she'd sanded them. Oily gunk all in her nails and everything scraped up. And stained terribly. In the end, I just painted them so the marks didn't show."

"Nails are so hard to keep perfect, but I have to admit I love it when they are." With warm satisfaction,

Mia watched the chips and breaks disappear from her nails. Janice held her hand in her soft cool one, meticulously erasing all imperfections.

"What color would you like today?" Janice asked, as she painted on the primer.

Mia looked at her pink tennis shoes. "Palest pink, I think. Just barely there."

"I have the perfect color," Janice said with a smile. "I'll go get it while you dry."

Mia leaned back in the soft chair, relaxing to the soothing sound of splashing water. She vaguely noticed a guest being ushered into the adjoining chair, then abruptly sat up when a cloying voice accosted her, "Mia, how are you, dear?"

Mandy settled herself in the chair, scooting her broad bottom back until she was firmly wedged into the chair. "I just had to try out your adorable little spa here."

"Hello, Mandy," Mia said. "I always love coming here. What treatments are you getting today?" Mandy certainly didn't need any more fillers, Mia thought, looking at the smooth plasticity of her face.

"Oh, just a mani and pedi and the tiniest touch up on my hair," Mandy said airily. "A massage too. All this stress," she sighed dramatically, resettling her spa robe.

Mia thought Mandy was getting as many treatments as she could fit in while Lauren was still paying the bill. "That sounds lovely. I hope you're enjoying your day."

"Oh, I am. I had to go into town this morning to

see Lauren's lawyer, you know," Mandy told her pretentiously. "It's such a lot of work being a trustee. Such a responsibility."

"You must be glad that will be over tomorrow then."

Mandy leaned toward her confidentially, "I'm not certain it will be over tomorrow." She shook her head in exaggerated sadness. "Poor Lauren's not well, as you know."

"Really?" Mia carefully kept the sarcasm from her tone.

"She might have to go to a mental home for a while." Mandy pursed her lips, her flabby jowls puffy. "You know?" She tried to look concerned, but her face remained frozen and expressionless.

"Oh dear," Mia privately thought Mandy was the one who belonged in a mental home.

Mandy's attendant clicked her tongue disapprovingly. "Mrs. Martin, your nails. They're in such bad shape. What ever did you do?"

Mandy hastily said, "All the boat rides and this rustic island." She sighed heavily. "They're just destroyed."

Another click from the attendant, "They definitely need to be wrapped."

Mandy nodded at her and turned back to Mia. "I heard Lauren is going around saying Paul was having an affair. I just can't believe that."

"But he was," Mia informed her with inward glee at the discomfiture on Mandy's face. "I saw the," she coughed, "incident. It was quite shocking." She shook

190

her head. "Terrible for Lauren to find out about the affair like that." She leaned closer, "Ms. Hathway's dress was half off, you know." She coughed again for emphasis.

"But..." Mandy's face fell, as much as it could.

"Lauren behaved very well under the circumstances, I think," Mia told her. "You should be proud of her."

"Huh," Mandy grunted, and her attendant led her away for her massage.

8

A Day Out

A dispirited group met at the dock for their company picnic outing. When they'd originally planned the evening clambake, Lauren thought it sounded like a wonderful treat. Now everyone was just standing around, looking at each other out of the corner of their eyes. She smiled in relief as Mia padded down the hill in a soft pink sweater and trim gray slacks. The hotel owner smiled and waved, seemingly completely oblivious of everyone else's uncomfortable expressions.

"It's been such a while since I went on a Maine clambake," Mia enthused. "Thank you so much for inviting me."

"I know," Lauren forced a lopsided smile. "We usually do a big company clambake every summer, but I'm always running around making sure everything runs smoothly. I thought for my birthday, I'd go on one where someone else did all the work." She kept her tight smile pasted on.

"What about everyone else?" Mia smiled brightly. No answers from the sullen group. "Do you go on regular picnic excursions like this, Courtney?" she directly asked, forcing the sulky woman to answer.

"We used to all the time when I was younger," Courtney's soft brown eyes misted a little, and she brushed her hair back from her face. "My mom made the most elaborate picnics ever, all out of whatever magazine she was reading. She would spread out this huge red and white checkered tablecloth, and it would be completely covered in food. It'd take ten trips to the car to get everything. And one trip back after we ate all the food in sight." She smiled, completely lost in her memory. "It was always a feast."

"How wonderful," Mia told her sincerely. "That's the sort of joyful occasion that's unforgettable."

"My mom really made my childhood special," Courtney smiled back at the older woman. "Maybe I'll make a picnic outing for her when it's really warm this summer. I'm sure she still has that tablecloth somewhere."

"You should," Mia encouraged. "Even if you pick up food from the deli, it will bring those cherished memories back and make some new happy ones."

"And take pictures to remember it," Lauren added. "I love looking through my old photos."

"I'm going to do that this summer," Courtney agreed, clearly looking forward to the event. "As soon as it gets warm enough for her to be outside."

Jeremy laughed suddenly, "Lauren, do you remember the time you had on that fancy dress for
194

that picnic so your mom could take pictures? And before she took any, you slipped on that rock and fell flat."

"Do I ever," Lauren grinned. "There was this green slime all over my white dress. I was dripping in it. It took at least five washes to come out. It was in my hair, all over my hands and legs. Absolutely awful."

"You looked like some kind of swamp creature, " Jeremy was laughing hard now. "We had to dunk you in the water so you could get clean enough to eat lunch."

"It was freezing that day too. I had the picnic blanket wrapped around me, shivering like crazy." Lauren added, "I still laugh every time I see those photos. I was trying to hide from the camera so hard, but my mom still took them."

"She was great," Jeremy added.

"Yeah, she was." They smiled fondly at each other.

Max laughed, "We didn't do many picnics, but my mom always did a fancy Sunday dinner every week after church. She still does, just a scaled down version for us both, and whoever happens to drop by. It's my favorite meal of the week. Plus, we eat the leftovers the first half of the week."

Lauren added, "You've got to try his mom's clam chowdah. It's seriously the best I've ever had."

When they stepped aboard the Picnic Boat, they were all vying with each other for family dinner stories. Mia smiled benevolently. She loved to see people enjoying a party. And if any group needed a nice outing, this group did. As she smiled at the stories, she noticed Cynthia, standing apart. She listened to the group with a serious frown on her face, not joining in the relaxing mood.

A cheerful group arrived at the small rocky beach on the deserted island the hotel used for clambakes. They were shuttled ashore in merry salt spray, and most of the party started off to explore the small island. The hospitality team began setting out tables and unfolding chairs for their feast.

Mia watched with interest as a huge metal box was ceremoniously lined with rocks, then fresh seaweed from the beach. Clams, mussels and lobsters were placed carefully inside, along with potatoes and fresh corn on the cob. The feast was covered in more seaweed, then a metal lid was fitted in place. The box was placed with a crunch on the fiery embers. Steam spouted, hissing from the edges as their meal cooked.

Cynthia stood staring blankly at the ocean for a minute, then slowly sat on a blanket on the beach, rolling the rounded rocks around with her fingers thoughtfully. Her highlighted hair stood stiffly in salt sprayed clumps, and her movements were uncertain and jerky. She looked upset.

Mia smoothly moved to sit down beside Cynthia. "Do you have any favorite family meals you used to do?" She smiled encouragingly.

Cynthia tugged her uncomfortably tight jeans down with sweaty palms and wiggled for a more comfortable seat on the slick dinosaur egg rocks. "No, no, I don't really. My mom worked long hours—she was a nurse. And my father travelled all the time, so we didn't really do many big family dinners."

Mia said with a commiserating smile, "Then I guess you missed the big family dinner dramas too."

"Yes, I guess," Cynthia trailed off. She said thoughtfully, twisting her bag handle around glossy orange nails, "You know, Lauren's parents were something special. I only really had a few conversations with them, but they were always so nice to me."

"I didn't realize you'd worked there that long," Mia smiled at her. "You must know everything about the company by now."

Cynthia nodded her head jerkily, "Oh yes, they hired me as a," she smiled in memory, "junior assistant accountant right out of college. I was very grateful to get a job back then, with no experience. I knew absolutely nothing, and they were so nice to train me. There weren't many jobs available when I graduated." She looked back over the years, lost in memories. "I gradually worked my way up through the accounting department."

"That's impressive," Mia encouraged. "It takes a lot of long hours to work your way up like that."

"Yes, a lot of long hours." Cynthia frowned a little, slightly sagging jowls tensing. "The company really means a lot to me after all these years."

"I can see why," Mia agreed easily.

"That's why I'm really worried about what's been going on. When I started running sales reports for Lauren, I," Cynthia broke off uncomfortably, her frown lines deepening. "You know, I think I need to speak with Lauren about it." She frowned, "Now isn't the time though."

Mia asked curiously, "What are you so worried about?"

"Oh, the murder, of course," Cynthia dismissed the question. "What else?"

Mia said thoughtfully, "You're the VP of finance. You know the company better than anyone."

Cynthia's lips compressed tightly, "I do." She said nothing else.

Mia knew it was useless to press her. "You really should help Lauren get up to speed, talk with her about your concerns. A lot's going on, and she needs your help. I know she'll need her help as she moves into her new responsibilities."

Cynthia nodded agreement, "I will. As soon as possible." She looked out over the endless ocean. "It'll be better to get it over with."

When it was obvious that was all Cynthia was going to say, Mia stood up. "I think I'll have a little stroll to explore the island before our feast. Would you like to come?"

Cynthia looked at her strappy sandals with mild distaste. "I really didn't bring the right shoes for this trip. I think I'll skip a twisted ankle and stay on the beach."

Mia looked at the roaring driftwood fire, bright sparks flying already. The wonderful aroma of steaming shellfish combined with the smoky scent of the fire. "I don't think it will be long before dinner. It's smelling delicious." She smiled at Cynthia, then walked up the beach to stretch her legs.

A more relaxed group showed up for the feast a few minutes later. They all, Cynthia included, posed for pictures in front of the backdrop of the fire and the sea. Jake and Blake, laughing, grabbed Courtney up and held her up in the air sideways for a photo. "We found a beautiful mermaid on the beach."

Courtney had lost her sour look. Laughing at being included in the fun, she faintly protested, "Hey, don't drop me, you guys!"

For a wonder, they put her down with gentle care and advanced on Cynthia. She shooed them away, smiling, "Go away, you two. Pick on someone else."

She smiled tolerantly at them, but didn't let them lift her. They continued their antics, leaping over the shorter side of the bonfire flames, singeing their sneakers.

Jeremy snapped photos like mad. "Don't worry, I'll edit out anything that looks bad," he assured them.

Lauren called, "Like me in green slime."

"Exactly." Jeremy continued to snap photos of the laughing group, warming their hands at the dancing fire. "Some memories are meant to last forever."

"Hey, remember capture the flag?" Jake grabbed a napkin off the table. "Catch me if you can!"

Blake lunged for him. Jake easily sidestepped him, but got a little too close to Max. With a laugh, Max leaned over and grabbed the napkin, "Mine!" He grinned widely, back to a boy playing games. He

199

darted off.

"Oh no, you don't," Lauren, laughing, grabbed for it as he passed, chasing Max around the table.

Jake and Blake joined the chase around the table, slipping and sliding on the round stones, Lauren still in the lead. Courtney made a cautious grab for the flag as Max ran by. Cynthia didn't even try, just smiled at the fun. The group went around and around the table, Max dancing just out of reach, continually in near collapse from laughter.

Lauren made a final lunge and snatched the napkin out of Max's belt, holding it up in triumph. "Mine!"

"Lauren!" a shrill voice pierced their laughter. "Have you gone mad? Why are you chasing that man? What's wrong with you?"

Their happy laughter ceased abruptly. A small dinghy pulled up on the shore, three passengers from a small boat moored next to their Picnic Boat.

With elaborate care, Paul helped Mandy Martin climb out of a small dinghy. She took mincing steps in her inappropriate shoes on the rolling beach rocks, an expression of disapproval on her face.

"Lauren, I can't believe you're running around like a crazy person at a time like this." Mandy shook her head in shocked disbelief. "I think Paul understated just how disturbed you've become. Attacking your employees. Really!" Her mouth pursed like a bubblegum ball. "Absolutely shocking display."

John Libby, left to clamber out of the small dinghy on his own, had a close call when his foot slipped on the round stones of the beach, but managed to wobble back upright. He slowly made his way up the beach, carefully feeling his way on the smooth stones. He cleared his throat, "Happy Birthday, Lauren. Paul said we should come to your party too. See what's going on." He frowned with disapproval.

"Happy Birthday, Lauren," Mandy called with brittle enthusiasm. "John and I thought, as your trustees," she smirked, "we should certainly come to your thirtieth birthday party. Paul was sweet enough to offer to bring us." She patted his arm with her plump, ring heavy hand.

Lauren's mouth hung open in surprise, then she abruptly closed it. She still held the white napkin high like a flag of surrender. "How nice, Mandy," she said insincerely, lips tight. "I'm so glad you both could come to my party. I didn't think you'd enjoy a clambake on the beach. I assumed you'd be dining at the hotel where you'd be more comfortable."

John made it up to the group, puffing hard. "Hi, young Lauren. Happy Birthday. So our trustee job might be done tomorrow. We wanted to check in, see how you are after the recent events." He nodded and collapsed into a nearby chair, bloated face panting and bright red. "What are you waving that napkin around for? Seems odd. Is there a reason?" He looked at her expectantly for more signs of madness, a sheen of sweat glossing his pate.

Lauren silently placed the napkin on the adjacent table.

Paul stood mockingly in front of the setting sun,

putting her in his shadow. "Miss me, Lauren dear?"

Max and Jeremy moved to stand protectively in front of Lauren. Their fists were balled and faces grim, far from the laughing boys of a few minutes ago.

She shook her head and moved to stand alone. Gritting her teeth, she said, "Paul, we're getting a divorce." She motioned to her trustees with a welcoming hand. "I'm very glad to see Mandy and John, of course," she managed to say with a straight face. "I hadn't planned on seeing them until tomorrow for my official signing. But why are you here?"

Max, standing immediately behind Lauren, stated firmly, "It's a company picnic, Paul. And Lauren's birthday party. You don't work for Tisserande anymore. And you know Lauren doesn't want to see you at her party after what happened." His fists were clenched, by his sides. His face was tense and set. His eyes sparkled with anger, looking like he might just enjoy a chance to fight.

"Who says?" Paul taunted, grinning. "Lauren doesn't have control of the company until her birthday tomorrow. And if she's in jail, she can't sign that paperwork, now, can she? So I'm in charge," he drew the last words out vengefully. He swayed and stumbled, then straightened up, swigging from a silver hip flask.

Mia wondered how many drinks Paul had had this afternoon. He seemed drunk, swaying on the round rocks.

Lauren's face was pale in the flickering firelight. "You're fired, Paul." Her voice broke a little. "Please leave."

Mandy broke in, sweet and cloying as syrup, "Now, you know if everyone stays calm, you two nice young people will work things out. Divorce is such an awful thing." She looked at Lauren, frozen face straining to appear sympathetic. "And Lauren, dear, if you're having," she coughed discretely, "mental issues, then you'll need Paul to guide the company while you're," she coughed again, "away for awhile."

"Excuse me?" Lauren's face clenched in sudden anger. "What exactly do you mean by that?"

John mumbled, "That woman, Melissa something, dying like that." He shook his head sorrowfully. "You can't possibly be responsible. Must have been an accident. Not your fault."

Lauren said through tight lips, "I am not responsible for Melissa Hathway's death."

"Of course not," Mandy said cloyingly. "I'm sure a good lawyer will make the court aware of your mental issues at the time. You'll just go for a nice rest cure for a bit and come back home. But of course, you can't possibly run the company from a mental hospital. So you need Paul. The last thing you need is a divorce." She sat down and smoothed her skirt complacently.

"I don't have mental issues, but I'm beginning to think you do." Lauren retorted sharply.

"Well, I never," broke in Mandy. She buffed her bubble gum pink nails on her skirt angrily, sharpening her claws.

Lauren talked over her burbling. "I'll be taking complete charge of my company tomorrow, on my birthday, as the trust states."

"Oh, I don't know if we should do that," Mandy demurred sweetly. "If you're found guilty, wouldn't it be better if Paul was running the company instead of you? Much better for the company's public image not to have a murderer, excuse me, a mental case, in charge. I do know a little more than you about business, sweetie."

"No," Lauren stated flatly. "And I will be getting outside accountants to audit everything starting tomorrow." She glared at her uninvited guests, clearly realizing for the first time they weren't necessarily well meaning bumblers. "Everything that has been done during the so-called trust will be gone over by an independent auditor," she added with decision, staring meaningfully at Mandy.

"Well, I never—" Mandy trailed off. "I'm sure Paul has been running Tisserande perfectly, no matter what any accountants say." Her jaw jutted out, eyes narrowing. "And, under the circumstances, I think you'd better let him continue."

"Now is not the time for this discussion. This is my birthday party. I'll meet you both tomorrow, at our scheduled appointment at Harvey's." Lauren shrugged, then relented slightly. "If you and John would like to stay for my birthday party, of course you are welcome." The last word was said through clenched teeth.

"I don't have to go anywhere." Paul made a wobbly gesture at the empty rocky beach. "It's a public island."

"It ain't public," Douglas spoke up, moving forward with a clomping stride in his huge rubber boots. "Owned by the hotel."

"Oh, well, then." Paul moved clumsily below the high tide mark of piled seaweed, straddling his feet wide to keep his balance. "Then I'll stay back here. I can't miss my darling wife's," he spat the word at Lauren, "thirtieth birthday party." He rubbed his hands together, gloating at his audience's faces.

"Well, really," Mandy pronounced. "You'd think after coming all this way, in that rotten little boat, you'd be glad to see us. It's not like freezing on a depressing beach is my idea of fun," she huffed.

"Seems odd," John peered at Lauren for any obvious signs of insanity. "You never did explain that napkin thing either." She glared back at him in silent fury.

"You didn't have permission to take my boat either," Douglas accused Paul.

Paul shrugged with elaborate ease, "I thought the boats were for hotel guests' use." He added bitingly, "Like the one my Melissa died on."

Douglas told him with decision, "You want to go on back, Mr. Baker. This is a private event."

"The lousy boat's broken. And this is my darling wife's big birthday party, out on some deserted rock. I'm here to celebrate." Paul rubbed his hands together and moved haltingly to inspect the long table. "Guess I'm staying for dinner, after all." Pulling out a comfortable looking chair, he collapsed into it, smirking. "Bring me a beer, okay? And make it cold." He grumbled, "Better be something besides damn fish for dinner, too."

Douglas muttered an inarticulate word, grabbed the dinghy and rowed it out to the runabout, jerking the oars at each dip. Tying it off, he clambered aboard. Mia watched him trying to start the small boat's engine with no result but coughs, then went over to Lauren.

Lauren's smile had gone brittle, like a glass veneer. She looked over at Mia, clearly on at her limit. "What do I do?" she asked the older woman softly.

Mia quietly advised, "I'd ignore him, dear. He's only doing this to irritate you. Don't let him get to you." She smiled reassuringly.

Lauren's face cracked a little. "Great advice, but not so easy to do."

"I know. Just try not to let him see it." Mia smiled kindly at her. "Do you want Douglas to shuttle him and your uninvited trustees back? He can do that, but it might keep us on the island a bit later than planned." She looked at Douglas working on the other boat. "It doesn't look like their boat is working, and I don't think Douglas will want them piloting it back, even if he can fix it."

"No, you're right." Lauren squared her shoulders and took a deep breath. "I'll just ignore him. And my so called trustees." She twisted her lips and whispered, "I know Mom just put Mandy on that trustee list to be nice. I wish Harvey hadn't been busy today. He called and said he and Tom couldn't come, at the last minute. I can't wait to get the company business and trust settled. And I'd much rather have them here than Mandy and John." She grinned lopsidedly, "Not that

Harvey's at his best on a picnic." She looked at the clambake preparations, "But what a picnic!"

Servers moved discretely around the table, pouring drinks. Long wooden boards with cheeses, baskets of crusty bread and grapes hanging over the sides were placed on the table. Mia noticed the busboy, Nick, carrying trays with exaggerated care and smiled in recognition. He winked back impishly, playing up his waiter role with an elaborate bow.

She smiled slightly at his antics, then looked thoughtfully out to sea. Douglas still hadn't been able to start the boat; it was coughing forlornly across the tide. Odd, the boat making it all the way to this island and then stopping dead. Almost as if it was planned by someone. She looked thoughtfully down the table at Paul, steadily drinking beer. Everyone said he didn't know anything about boats, but he had certainly seemed comfortably skilled at piloting a small craft to exactly where he wanted to be. She wondered why he had come. Just to ruin Lauren's birthday party, or a more nefarious motive?

She did a quick hostess glance up and down the table. Lauren had settled back in her chair, quietly toying with a piece of bread. Max's plate was piled high with the cheese board offerings. He attacked his food with darting glances at Paul as he bit into the bread with strong white teeth. Courtney was still half smiling, sitting between Jake and Blake. She pointedly addressed her remarks to her companions and Jeremy, completely ignoring Paul. Cynthia hovered on the edge of the group, unsure where she fit in.

Mia called out, "Cynthia!" She motioned the woman to come over to sit between her and Lauren.

Cynthia awkwardly perched on the edge of a chair, like an emu contemplating flight. She took off her glasses and polished them. Her eyes appeared dimly unfocused without the bright orange frames. "Yes, Mia?" she asked, her voice tremulous.

Mia chattily continued, "Cynthia was just telling me about when she first came to work at Tisserande and how nice your parents were." She sipped her champagne, savoring the dry fizz on her tongue.

Lauren said, "That's right—you'd been there a few years when they died, hadn't you? So you knew Mom and Pop?"

Cynthia's smile left her eyes still worried, clearly she was trying to do her social duty to be cheerful at a rather awkward birthday party. "Yes, Tisserande was my very first job out of college. You wouldn't believe how little I knew about business back then."

"Yes, real life is a lot different than they teach in college, isn't it?" Lauren agreed. "I can't count how many mistakes I made when I started working at the company. I didn't have a clue how to apply my knowledge. And I didn't know enough!" They smiled, remembering frustrations.

"The first supplies report I turned in was exactly like my professor had taught. Textbook perfect, I think I even copied the format from my textbook." Cynthia's brow wrinkled and she pursed her lips in embarrassed memory. "Your mom had to take it apart and put it back together for me, explaining so nicely how what

208

I'd given was not the relevant information she'd asked for at all. I was mortified," her face went a little pink at the memory, "but she was so nice about it." She grimaced, "The next report, she called me to her office."

"Oh no," Lauren exclaimed, holding her hands up to her face in horror.

"I was petrified that I was being fired for messing up again, but she called me in to tell me I'd done it perfectly." Cynthia laughed, her tone a little shrill. "And she gave me cookies to celebrate." She giggled. "She'd actually baked cookies for me."

"That was my mom. She always celebrated with cookies." Lauren's smile was wide.

"She baked them for every possible occasion at work, I know that." Cynthia's eyes grew dreamy, "They were those really gooey ones with chocolate chunks and caramel in them. My mouth still waters at their memory."

"I have the recipe, if you like," Lauren told her with a grin. "Or I might make them. I hadn't thought about those cookies in years. They were really good."

Cynthia laughed, "Me either." She looked intently at Lauren, then spoke quickly, as if trying to get the words out before she changed her mind, "I need to meet with you about some things tomorrow, if you don't mind." She glanced down at the table toward Paul and quickly back, not meeting Lauren's eyes.

Lauren looked at her curiously, "Sure, Cynthia. Whenever you want."

"I think the sooner the better," Cynthia's lips compressed, eyes darting quickly down the table at the others. Her hand tightened on her wine glass, orange nails digging into her skin. "I really need to see you tomorrow."

"Of course," Lauren agreed. Then she laughed and held up her glass. "I can't promise to have the cookie recipe ready yet, though. I'll have to look through my mom's old recipe box at home for those. Then we'll bake them."

"Not in your lab, we won't," Cynthia retorted with a grin. "Around all those chemicals is no place for food."

They laughed, clinking glasses, then both jumped as Paul suddenly leaned in between them with his beer glass. "Having fun, ladies?" He wobbled unsteadily, propping himself up on Cynthia and Lauren's chairs. Mia wondered just how many beers he'd had on his boat before he'd crashed the party.

He openly jeered at their startled jumps, then swayed away, drink in hand, as Max stood up, his loose arms ready for a fight.

Paul held up his arms in mock defense, swaying a little, "Just wanted to let you know Douglas there says my boat might have been tampered with." He smirked and wiped his mouth with the back of his hand. "Tampered with. Just like poor Melissa's, huh? Guess I'm definitely here for the big birthday party. Should be a night to remember." He weaved away, snickering at their discomfiture.

Lauren shook her head in disbelief, brushing her hair back from her face. "Why didn't I get a divorce years ago?"

"Pure stubbornness," Max told her, patting her shoulder briefly as he sat back down. "It's just like you to try to make impossible things work."

"I guess," Lauren stared in disgust at Paul guzzling down his beer and shook her head incredulously. "Well, it'll be over soon."

Max said easily, looking straight into her eyes, "We all make at least one mistake."

She looked down at the tablecloth, reddening, smiling a little to herself.

Cynthia pursed her lips tightly. "Relationships are complicated. We don't always do what we know is best." She looked out over the dark sea, beyond their small circle of warm firelight, tugging her sweater closer around her.

Mia broke in cheerfully, "Driftwood always makes the most colorful fires, doesn't it?"

"The violet flames are from potassium chloride, green from sodium chloride," Lauren said dreamily. "All kinds of odd effects happen with driftwood since you never know what minerals it will pick up in the briny."

"I love having a wood fire in the winter," Cynthia said, now smiling at the leaping flames. "Nothing else is quite the same."

"I agree," Lauren said. "I keep a huge pile in the shed. I always have a kettle ready for the wood stove in the kitchen too."

Mandy minced her way over to Lauren, trying not to stumble on the slippery beach rocks. "I do so want you to have a happy birthday, sweetie." She gave

211

Lauren a stiff kiss on the cheek. "I don't want you to worry about one little thing."

John lumbered behind Mandy, "Happy birthday, Lauren." His round cheeks were red. "I know everything is going to be fine. Don't worry, we'll take good care of you. Keep you safe." He patted her hand heavily with an oily hand.

"Thank you." Lauren's face was blank. When they had shuffled on, she discreetly wiped her hand on her napkin, expression blank. She stared after them, as if trying to decipher the meaning behind their actions.

Holding up her champagne glass, Mia quietly toasted, "To the next stage of life—it's going to be the best one yet."

Lauren blushed and smiled her lopsided smile, clinking her glass with Mia's and sipping. She refocussed on the people around her, smiling back at the group surrounding her with love and friendship. Max's eyes were dancing with merry enjoyment, Jeremy still looked concerned, but the lines around his mouth were starting to relax. Cynthia smiled back at her, holding up her glass, "To Lauren!" Jake and Blake thumped the table in emphasis.

"To good friends and family," Lauren returned the toast, now smiling with pure enjoyment. "Thank you all so much for coming. It's going to be a great year!"

"And a great dinner!" Max added, sniffing as the servers lined up with their feast.

With pride, Nick placed a huge platter of steamers and mussels on the table, along with more baskets of bread. Mia noticed Douglas standing on the shore. He stood off to the side, looking at the group with a frown. He noticed her curious gaze, and gave her a sharp nod, telegraphing things were under control at his end. He'd found chairs somewhere for the unwanted extra guests, placing them at the far end of the long table. She noticed the runabout was tied to the Picnic Boat, ready to be towed behind when they left.

Mia looked away from Douglas, not wanting the guests to worry about boat tampering. She knew Douglas would check their boat thoroughly before he allowed them aboard. No one could have sabotaged it since they arrived, in any case. She was sure Paul had disabled the runabout to be stuck here, which meant he knew a lot more about boats and engines than he'd admitted to. Even if Douglas could fix the small boat here, he couldn't let guests pilot it after any failures. There wasn't much to do about the situation except try to let Lauren have the birthday party she'd wanted.

"This looks delicious!" she enthused at the feast.

"It does indeed," Jeremy scooped up his shellfish and broke off a hunk of bread for dipping with obvious pleasure. "I love trying new things, but a classic clambake is not something to mess around with. It's perfection just like it is."

Mia delicately ate the clams and mussels, restraining herself from making the full meal from them alone. This was just the start of the feast. The slight tang of salty umami from seaweed combined with the smoky flavor from the fire into a blissful experience.

Silence reigned, broken only by the clink of discarded shells and waiters refilling glasses. Even Jeremy ate quietly, concentrating wholeheartedly on the food.

While they were still eating the clams, they were served fish chowder in rough clay bowls. The creamy broth was flavored with salt pork, hearty chunks of fish, potatoes and onions. Mia inhaled the smoky fish aroma and took a bite. Her eyes met Lauren's as they both said, "Mmm."

Two platters of bright red lobsters was placed on the table, with plenty for all. Jake and Blake grabbed for them at the same time, drawing back hot fingers at the same moment long tongs were placed on the platter. After a brief scuffle, Jake snagged the first lobster and Blake the second. Blake then laughingly appointed himself waiter, shooing away Nick, trying to do his job. He placed one of the red crustaceans by every diner's place, waggling its claws in pinching motions, then circled around to his place, grinning. Nick handed out the obligatory drawn butter in red ramekins.

Mia heard Mandy whining to Paul, "Why Lauren can't have her birthday dinner in a nice restaurant like everyone else, I don't know. It's so unnatural." Mandy tightened her expensive jacket around her shoulders and dramatically shivered.

Paul didn't reply, grabbing another lobster off the tray, mouth shiny with butter. He topped off his beer from his flask, pouring a lot of whatever he was

214

fortifying it with, from what Mia could see.

Against the soft background music of lapping waves, there were sounds of the fire crackling, crunch of the lobster shells and scraping of bowls. "You know the food is really good," Max commented with a smile, "when no one's talking." He addressed himself to his bowl of chowder.

Jeremy waved an ear of corn, "Hear, hear."

"I can't hear anything," Lauren grinned. "This is so good." She glowed with happiness again, a woman celebrating her birthday and the start of a new year of life.

After the feast, everyone sat around the roaring campfire, moving chairs around to get just the right distance from the blazing heat. Mugs of hot chocolate topped with foamy cream and glasses of wine were placed on convenient little tables. Mia cheerfully continued to sip her preferred champagne.

When the plates of graham crackers, chocolate and marshmallows with a toasting fork were handed out for s'mores, there were a lot of murmurs of "I couldn't possibly," but everyone except Mandy took one.

Mandy dragged her chair back from the fire, then shivered, moving it back next to Cynthia's. She looked with longing at the s'mores everyone else was enjoying, but refused to stoop to asking for one. "I thought you'd have a birthday cake at least, Lauren," she observed with a disapproving frown.

Lauren laughed happily, "Oh, I thought s'mores would be so much fun. Like summer camp." She stood next to the fire, turning her marshmallow in the heat.

Firelight danced on faces as they concentrated on getting their marshmallows to the perfect consistency. Some liked theirs perfectly light brown, like Mia, and some created flaming torches, like Jeremy. Happy contentment reigned in the sticky faces and fingers. Lauren leaned back against her chair, completely relaxed. "What a great birthday. Thanks for being here, you guys."

Max briefly squeezed her shoulder. "Next year will be even better."

"Absolutely," Jeremy added, smiling.

"Next year you'll be in jail, honey," Paul snarled drunkenly, suddenly towering over the group, beer in hand. He coughed loudly. Everyone jumped.

Swaying over Jeremy, Paul spilled beer on Jeremy's pants. Jeremy abruptly stood up, looking like he wanted to punch Paul. Wordlessly, Courtney pulled him back, clinging to his arm.

They'd forgotten Paul, still quietly drinking himself drunk at the table. "You're going to jail, baby. And never ever coming back out." He grabbed the drinks table for balance, making glasses clink when he thunked his down."Murdering bitch!" Jeremy and Courtney quickly rescued bottles and glasses as they swayed.

"And every one of you will be fired. By me." He pointed his shaking finger like a gun, punctuating his threat with a trigger click. He smiled at their faces, white in the orange glow. "That's right," he smirked, swaying on his feet. "The trustees are on my side, not hers. Right, Mandy?" He pointed at John and Mandy, sneering down at Lauren, "They can't afford to be on your side, darling."

"Well, really," Mandy complained, voice as brittlely sweet as cotton candy. "I don't know what he could possibly mean by that."

Mia heard Max murmur, "Don't you?" She looked at him quickly, but he was looking at Lauren.

John added ponderously, "Whatever happens, he shouldn't talk like that at your birthday party. I think he's had just a bit too much to drink." He nodded his head slowly. "It's been an upsetting time."

"You think?" Max commented under his breath. He gave John a disgusted look.

Paul leaned down and abruptly threw a log hard onto the fire. The leaping flames showered the group in sparks. Everyone got up in a hurry, frantically brushing ashes and sparks off. Laughing in uncontrolled glee, his unsteady figure just stood there, watching them scatter away from the fire. He threw another log in, jeering as they backed off.

"Now Paul," Cynthia gingerly placed her hand on his sleeve, "You need to be more careful."

"Oh, Cynthia, be careful," he mocked, looking angrily down at her. Beads of sweat poured down his forehead. "You'll do whatever I say. Whatever I say."

Mandy suddenly screeched, "My skirt!" A tiny wisp of smoke rose where a spark had lodged. She screamed again, running around wildly, then crashed to the ground, pudgy legs crumpling, skirt hiked up, revealing substantial underwear. The spark on her skirt had extinguished itself almost immediately.

"Are you okay?" They all ran to help her up.

"My ankle!" Mandy wailed. Jake and Blake pulled a chair over, hauling her up and gently settling her into it. She basked at the young male attention. When they thoughtfully brought her a s'more, she didn't refuse it this time, smiling up at them in what she clearly thought was an alluring manner.

Mia looked at Mandy's ankle. Mandy had seemed undecided about which ankle was hurt for a minute, then settled on her right one. Of course, with high heels on a rocky beach, it was just a matter of time before she really did twist it. Mia wasn't buying it this particular time though. She took an appreciative bite of her s'more.

The distraction had defused Paul's anger. He found a chair near the fire where he and his supplemented beer sat, silently brooding, wiping beads of sweat off his forehead.

Lauren said defiantly, "Well, guys, we're not letting that spoil our party, are we?"

"Of course not," Mia encouraged loudly.

"Don't worry about me," Mandy giggled up at her cavaliers. "I'll be fine." Mia noticed Jake putting quite a lot of brandy in her hot chocolate mug. He winked at Mia as he saw her looking.

"Let's give Paul a few minutes to pass out," Lauren said quietly. "He'll be easier to manage when he's asleep."

"That way we don't have to deal with him on the trip back," Jeremy completed with relish. "We will have
218

to carry him, though. Hopefully for the last time. I thought he'd break my back last company Christmas party."

Lauren made a disgusted face, but said nothing. What Paul did was no longer her problem, she seemed to feel.

"Good plan," Max agreed, propping his legs up to warm at the fire. "Anyone know a good ghost story?"

They all laughed, but no one volunteered.

Tension gradually relaxed around the group. John fell asleep, snoring loudly, sound only slightly muffled by his blanket. Mandy drank her spiked hot chocolate, looking petulantly at her tight burnt skirt, while Jake told her elaborately gestured stories. They seemed to involve a lot of football throws, from what Mia could see.

They talked together, enjoying the firelight. Courtney, Mia and Jeremy moved a further away from the fire to see the stars better. "I love looking at the stars," Courtney said, gazing upward. "We're only a little way out from the mainland, but I think you can see twice as many out here."

"It's staggeringly gorgeous," Mia agreed, leaning back in her chair to see better. "I'm afraid the only one I recognize is the Big Dipper."

"It's been a long time since my Scout days," Jeremy demurred, but pointed up into the sky. "You can follow that back to Orion." He leaned close to Courtney, pointing constellations out.

Mia smiled benevolently, looking up into the deep bowl of the night sky. The fire was down to soft embers now, barely glowing. Starlight glistened on the surface of the waves, slapping on the rounded beach rocks, hissing softly as the water drew back. The smell of smoke and iodine whiffs of seaweed drifted through the air. Murmured laughter rang out from the other little groups and the occasional ooh of delight as Courtney spotted another constellation with Jeremy's inexpert guidance.

A harsh gasp for air suddenly broke into the tranquil scene. Paul stood up, knocking over his chair. His hands clawed his throat, eyes wide in panic. Gasping for breath, he spasmed and threw up into the fire, embers sizzling. His legs spasmed, kicking rocks to the side. He pointed into the shadows beyond the fire, screaming in a harsh call, "You..." but could say no more. Agonized eyes suddenly fought for life, face flickering in and out of focus in the firelight.

Max and Jeremy ran to Paul, supporting him between them. "Are you choking?" Jeremy yelled as Max pounded on his back.

Paul managed to shake his head once, then clawed at the air and his throat, desperately trying to get air. He hung from the two men, unable to support himself. His body spasmed and they lowered him to the ground. His head banged on the rocks, uncontrollably spasming.

Mia yelled, "Call an ambulance!" Grabbing a cushion, she ran to hold Paul's head off the rocks. Paul's eyes closed and he stopped moving. Mia felt for a pulse. "He's not breathing. Quick!"

Max knelt beside Paul, beginning chest

compressions. After a minute, he switched off with Jeremy.

"Paul! Paul! You've got to try. Come on, Paul. Breathe!" The group huddled around him, exhorting him to live, just try to breathe. Lauren stood, eyes huge in horror, watching her husband die in front of her.

Paul lay there, unmoving, like a sack of flour being pummeled by Max and Jeremy. They tried one more round of compressions, then another round, slowing down the frantic rush, now expecting no response. Mia felt his pulse for what seemed the thousandth time. "Nothing."

Jeremy stood up and kicked a round rock, skittering it into the smoldering fire where it trailed sparks. Max felt for the pulse himself, closing his eyes as he tried to feel something under his fingers. He shook his head and sat back on his heels. "Nothing," he agreed. He thumped the chest again, hard.

"Did he have a heart attack?" Lauren asked with wide eyes. "He didn't have heart problems."

"I don't know," Max frowned at Paul's body. "I don't know what happened."

They heard the distant roar of a helicopter in the dark night sky, too late to save Paul.

9

Lost At Sea

The helicopter blades spun slowly, whipping the fire into hot flames. Bright light shone in strobed flashes on scared faces. Courtney's eyes showed the whites; dark hair thrashed her face. Jeremy stood beside her. His mouth hung open, shoulders slack in exhausted shock.

Max, body tight in hurry, helped the paramedics load Paul's still form onto the stretcher. The paramedics felt for his pulse, slowing down their frantic rush when none was found. They strapped his stretcher into the carrier, pointlessly going through the motions of rescue.

As the helicopter flew off, they were left in the uncertain flames of the dying fire. Douglas jumped as his handheld radio squawked, "Yes?"

Shrill grating sounds, gradually resolving into a clearer connection to a woman's voice. "...there. I repeat, do not leave the island... Do you understand?

Under no circumstances are you to leave the island. Awk!" the radio dissolved into buzzes and squawks.

Douglas answered, briefly cutting into the static noise, "We'll remain on the island. What's your ETA?"

Nothing. Just the buzzing of a bad signal.

Mia said solemnly, "I'm sure they won't be long. We're fine waiting until they arrive." She looked around the group, assessing them.

Lauren stood off to one side, shivering uncontrollably. Max glanced at her, then went over, wrapping her in his arms. Her arms spasmed, then wrapped around him for support, knuckles white as they held on to him. Her shocked face was blank, eyes wide in horror.

Jake and Blake sat in their chairs by the fire, quiet for once. They stared into the fire embers, identical in their collapsed state.

John lay sluggishly in his chair, frowning at the ground. Mandy sat beside him, trying to hide her glee at the drama. She swung her chubby leg impatiently, ersatz hurt ankle forgotten. Mia saw her lips moving, planning her story for the police and her luncheon gossip for months to come.

Douglas frowned out at the horizon, searching for the lights of a police boat. He paced in his tall rubber boots at the water's edge, darting quick suspicious glances at the group around the fire.

Nothing could be heard but the brittle crackle of the dying fire and the waves softly slapping against the rocky shore. They all stared into nothing, awed by Paul's sudden death.

Lauren slid to her knees on the rocky shore, unable to stand even with Max's arms. "Why would anyone want to kill Paul? He was leaving. Why would anyone want to kill him?" she whispered, trapped in a desperate loop.

Max said quietly, "He might have had a heart attack or something."

"He told me his heart was fine after his last physical," Lauren said dully.

No one replied.

Mia doubted it had been a heart attack. Paul's death had been quick and violent. Her own guess was poison. "Lauren, you need to pull yourself together," she told her firmly. "Chief White will be questioning everyone soon."

Lauren didn't seem to hear, leaning into Max's arm. That wouldn't do, Mia thought. She tugged on Max's other arm to get his attention. Mia ordered, "Max, you need to build up the fire." He looked up, startled, then nodded agreement, still not moving away from Lauren. She called out, "Jeremy, Jake, Blake, build up the fire. We need warmth and light."

Mia briefly considered hot drinks all around, deciding that would not be smart. They didn't know yet what had killed Paul, but something he ate or drank tonight would be a very good bet. She shivered a minute, wondering whose hand had held poison.

Moving robotically, the men did as she asked, carrying bundles of driftwood and building the fire. They piled the wood high in their relief at being given a definite task to accomplish. Bright flames lit the barren beach, heat radiating toward the numb group. Chairs were pulled up to the fire, huddling close for warmth in the dark night.

Courtney put shaking hands up, her delicate fingers looking translucent against the firelight, absorbing the heat. "Poor Paul," she said dully. "What an awful way to go."

"Poor Paul," Jeremy agreed, putting his hands up to feel the fire. Flames flickered in his face, bright then briefly shadowed. His mouth sagged downward in shock. He placed his hand on Courtney's, gently patting it, and she looked at him with a startled glance and burst into loud tears.

Mia went over to her. "Courtney, dear, that's not going to help." She patted Courtney's shoulder. "We have to stay calm."

Courtney cried harder, fists balled against her eyes. "I can't believe Paul's dead. Dead. Right in front of us." She rubbed her temples in a circular motion.

"I know, it's a tremendous shock," Mia's voice stayed levelly smooth. "But you need to stay calm and be ready to talk with the police." She dragged her chair over to beside Courtney and held her hand, trying to prevent Courtney from collapsing. "There's nothing we can do right now to help Paul." She wondered at the woman's grief. It seemed excessive for a man she appeared to dislike, but Courtney had clearly been at her limit for some time.

Lauren had been staring straight ahead at the fire, freezing beneath the warm blanket wrapped tightly around her. "Oh, why did he come here

226

tonight?" she said dully, then remembered. "If he hadn't come, maybe he'd still be alive." Tears started flowing from her unresponsive face. "Maybe they'll be able to help him at the hospital." Even she didn't believe that. Tears flowed smoothly down her expressionless face, then her calm mask collapsed into grief. "Oh, he can't really be dead. I wanted him gone, out of my life, not dead. Oh, Paul." She twisted her shaking hands together in a knot, shaking uncontrollably.

Courtney cried out, "He was poisoned. He must have been. First Melissa, then Paul. I don't want to be next!" Her fine boned hands shook, red nails shining in the flaring flames. "I don't know anything!"

Jeremy made a move toward her, then stopped himself abruptly, sagging back. He leaned toward the fire, face bright from the intense heat. His feet scuffed against the rocks, coating his shoes in soot.

They all sat there by the leaping flames in silence, each trying not to meet anyone else's eyes. Mia could see the thought growing in their eyes. One of their small group was a murderer. Who?

With relief, Douglas called out from the shore, "Police boat coming." He walked quickly over to meet the police zodiac roaring to the island.

Chief White cumbrously hauled himself out of the boat and walked up the rocky shore. "So, you folks killed off another person. Two murders now." It was not a question. His face was beet red with annoyance of having to come out here, at night, to a deserted island. He put his hands on his hips, obviously antagonistic.

He looked at Mia, "So what's your hotel serving for picnics now? Arsenic in the pâté?" He drew out the last word with a sneer.

Mia replied acerbically, "It was a classic Maine clambake."

"Ayuh. Anyone cooking it not a flatlander?" He snorted disgustedly, puffing out red cheeks. "Maine clambake? Hah." He stomped over to the fire, going on, "So her husband just drops down dead in the middle of dinner?"

Lauren said softly, "He is dead, then? We couldn't find a heartbeat, but we hoped the hospital..." she trailed off.

"Ayuh. Of course he's dead," Chief White said bluntly. "Dead on arrival. We strongly suspect poison. We'll know which one after the autopsy." He gave a harsh bark. "Not surprising, under the circumstances. Murder seems to happen around you." He glared vindictively at Lauren. "First your husband's lover, now your husband. Doesn't take a rocket scientist to know who killed them," he spat at her.

"Oh!" Courtney covered her eyes with her hands, blotting out the news.

"So none of you has any chance to drop the poison in the ocean on the way back, we're searching you for it here," the chief continued pugnaciously. "We'll search you, then you can go back to your fancy hotel rooms." He glared at Lauren, "Last night you'll have in a decent bed for a while, I'll tell you that."

"I'm fine with you searching me," Lauren said,

her arms hanging helplessly at her sides. "You won't find anything."

"Already hid the poison, huh? Well, my men will find it."

"Well, you're not strip searching me on some freezing rock in the middle of the ocean!" Mandy refused. "Why would I want to poison some man I hardly knew anyway?" Her hands were set firmly on her hips in defiance.

"Why would you, one of Lauren's trustees, want to poison Tisserande's CEO, whom you personally hired?" Max asked in a soft but penetrating voice. "I can't imagine."

Chief White looked up quickly, dark eyes darting suspiciously to Mandy. "One of Mrs. Baker's trustees?"

Mandy nodded emphatically, "I had nothing to do with anyone dying." She wrinkled her nose. "Paul said we needed to come and see how crazy Lauren was, so we could commit her. Lock her away where she couldn't hurt anyone else." She smirked at Lauren, clearly playing her winning card. "This proves he was right." Her look at Lauren was pure hatred.

The chief nodded, eyes moving from Lauren to Mandy. "I think we'll search you here, all the same. Here or at the jail, your choice."

Mandy's arms moved to hug her body close. "I can't go to jail!" she cried. She said dispiritedly, "Fine, then here. I'll get it over with."

"Good choice," Chief White said, moving on.

The rest nodded agreement. No one really cared what happened to Mandy.

They separated out, a policewoman searching the women behind a hastily strung up tarp. It was freezing in the cold night away from the warmth of the fire. The short, stocky woman had everyone strip down to their underwear and pawed through their clothes, looking for anything that could have contained poison. She kept looking up at them distrustfully.

Mia stood shivering in her delicate pink Chantilly lace lingerie under a scratchy gray wool blanket. "I don't know about you all, but I'm looking forward to a long hot shower." She smiled reassuringly at Courtney and Lauren, both wrapped tightly in their inadequate blankets. Cynthia stood like a statue wrapped in her stiff blanket, her gaunt body shuddering uncontrollably, her lips turning blue. Despite her ample natural padding, Mandy whined constantly about the cold and how uncomfortable she was.

The police woman stolidly left Mandy's clothes until the very last, returning them with seeming reluctance. She must have really thought she would find something there, Mia mused.

They dressed in record time in the chill air, then were hustled onto the picnic boat.

"Well," Mandy said with asperity, "It's some birthday party you planned."

Lauren finally broke her calm. "This is not entertainment, Mandy. Paul is dead," she said harshly, still shaking under the scratchy gray blanket. "Paul's dead," she repeated, almost reverently.

The beach behind them was covered in

temporary lights, with police officers moving around purposefully. The fire had been allowed to die down. A constable cautiously stirred the ashes with a long metal pole, searching for half burnt evidence.

The ride back was a frigid nightmare. They weren't allowed below in the warm cabin. The police boat followed them with its spotlight glaring on the other boat, to see their every move. Weird shadows sprang up as they bounced in the waves, motions not quite in sync. Paul's boat bobbed at the end of a strained line, awkwardly tethered. Two police, the woman who had searched them and another man, crowded onto the boat deck, glaring at them with suspicion. The Picnic Boat, while a fairly large boat, was feeling very crowded at this point. No one could drop anything overboard without being seen by at least two police now.

They arrived back at past two in the morning, bumping the dock with less grace than Douglas usually showed. Max jumped on the dock, efficiently tying the dock lines off, then helped the women as they clambered off the boat. He tried to give the police woman a helping hand, but she gave him a look clearly telegraphing that she'd shove him in the water if he didn't leave her alone.

A cold, miserable group straggled back to the hotel. As they herded toward the elevators, heading towards hot showers and warm clothes, Chief White bellowed into the still hotel, "No one is to leave this island. I'll be back to question each and every one of you in the morning." He emphasized, "Especially Mrs.

231

Baker." He glared at Lauren, who looked back with silent exhaustion.

"I wonder why Paul came tonight?" Cynthia suddenly asked.

Chief White pounced, "What do you mean?"

"He wasn't invited to Lauren's birthday party," Cynthia explained. "I wonder why he decided to crash it."

"Your birthday party?" Chief White quizzed Lauren.

"Yes," Lauren answered softly. She looked out the dark window. "Today is my thirtieth birthday. I assume control of Tisserande today." Her shoulders slumped under the new weight already.

"Hah. Maybe some new policies will keep the rest of Megeso Point from being fired," Chief White nodded with approval. "Your husband told me he stood firmly against you closing down the rest of the business, but you were going to fire everyone anyway."

Lauren's mouth hung open, then snapped close to a thin line.

The chief continued, with a wily smile, "I doubt you will have time for business meetings tomorrow. You're going to be busy answering my questions all day long." He smirked. "And you'd better enjoy your night in this fancy hotel too. Tomorrow night, you'll be sleeping in my jail."

Shoulders straightening, Lauren returned with quiet dignity, "Whether or not you believe me, Chief White, I am saving my town. I didn't kill Paul. And I'll make it my first priority tomorrow to finish my trust paperwork and make arrangements for Jeremy, Max and my lawyer, Harvey, to take over in case I can't," she choked a minute, "run things for a while." She glared at Chief White. "Taking care of my company is my only job tomorrow, and I can do it from jail if I have to." She added defiantly, "Harvey already has the papers drawn up. All I have to do is sign on the dotted line, order a full audit and put the people I trust in charge."

Chief White shrugged, bulldog eyes glaring at Lauren. "Not my business, unfortunately, what you're going to do with your inherited company. Or who you're going to fire first. But plan on some long talks with me tomorrow. And you might need a criminal lawyer, not your fancy corporate one." On that note, he marched out the door.

Mandy asked warily, "You're really getting Tisserande audited, Lauren? But why ever? We had accountants checking it out every other year."

Lauren answered shortly, "Because I'm not sure what's been going on there under Paul's watch, but I know I'm going to find out."

Mandy breathed out, "Ooh," with a wincing breath. For once, she didn't seem to have anything else to say. She took the first elevator, barely remembering to hobble on her hurt ankle. John bobbed behind, looking back at Lauren with round disapproving lips. Cynthia followed them into the elevator, thin arms hugging herself and frowning in concentration.

Mia took hold of Lauren's elbow, guiding her firmly into the next elevator. Max and Jeremy followed tightly behind them. They herded Lauren to her room, then shut the door.

Mia perched on the elegant armchair next to the fire. The group gathered around her, Lauren pulling the lap blanket up around her on the sofa.

Mia began, "I know we're all ready for baths and bed." She smiled ruefully, "I certainly am. But Paul's death narrows the field of suspects considerably." She took a deep breath. "Lauren, I'm very sorry Paul died like that. I can't imagine a worse way for a marriage to end."

Lauren huddled miserably under the blanket. "Yeah, now I feel guilty for hating him so much. I really wanted him out of my life, but not like this."

Mia patted her hand, then coughed slightly. "I have to admit when he showed up on a boat with convenient engine problems tonight, I was sure he had killed Melissa. I'm sorry, Lauren. I was clearly wrong."

"The suspects are now just us," Lauren said, sagging back into the sofa and pulling the blanket tighter.

"Not just us," Max objected. "Frankly, I thought Paul was the guilty one too. He's the only one who seemed capable of murder." He darted a look at Lauren, then shifted his eyes away. "I just couldn't understand why he'd kill Melissa."

"You never told me that," Lauren's eyes narrowed.

Max held out his hands. "I didn't know anything," he wiggled uncomfortably, "I didn't have any proof he was guilty. And I guess his death exonerates him. Paul didn't kill anyone."

"Yeah," Lauren's face said she'd thought Paul was guilty too, but she would never admit aloud she'd thought her husband of eight years could be a murderer. She looked down at her hands tightly gripping the blanket.

Max looked down too. "Yes, well, the same someone who killed Melissa must have killed Paul." He sighed heavily. "I really don't think it's one of us three. Or Mia, since she just met us this week." He shifted his weight on the sofa uncomfortably.

Mia said with finality, "Who then?" She counted off the possible suspects, "It has to be someone at the party. So Mandy, John, Cynthia, Jake, Blake and Courtney. I don't think my hospitality team is involved, though they are local," she added circumspectly.

Jeremy added hopefully, "Unless he committed suicide."

"Would Paul commit suicide at a party?" Mia looked at Lauren questioningly.

Lauren stared at her hands, knuckles white.

"It seems out of character," Max told Mia. "Frankly, I think he was too selfish to commit suicide." His hands tightened on his knees. "I really don't see him swallowing poison at a birthday party, far from hospitals. Paul might have done something as a stunt to gain sympathy or deflect suspicion, but not anything that had a chance of actually killing him. He certainly wouldn't have sat there silently while it was working."

"No," Mia agreed. "He didn't seem the suicidal

type." She shook her head. "Of course, it could have been a heart attack, an aneurysm, something like that. He must have been under a fair amount of stress with his marriage and job ending at the same time."

"I just can't believe he's dead," Lauren said, pulling the soft blanket tightly around her.

Mia patted her arm, "I'm sorry, dear. Even if you were divorcing him, a death is a terrible way to end a marriage. You were married for eight years? That's a long time."

"It seems like forever," Lauren sounded defeated, huddled under her blanket, face hidden by her dark hair.

Jeremy offered another theory, "Is it possible he was killed by accident?"

"He was the only one drinking beer," Mia said. "Of course, poison could have been put in his food, his flask or a pill. If it was a pill or his flask, someone not at the party could have given it to him. Anyone really." She personally still thought the suspect pool was pretty tight.

"What kind of poison would kill him like that?" Max asked.

"What exactly killed him?" Jeremy asked, looking up. "He looked like he was choking. Then like a heart attack, so we did the compressions."

They continued discussing possible poisons. Since none of them had ever planned to kill anyone, their deductions didn't go very far.

Suddenly Lauren stood up. "His laptop. I want to see Paul's laptop."

"It must be in his room. The police will let us have it back eventually." Max added succinctly, "Company laptop."

"Why do you want it, Lauren?" Mia asked.

"I just feel like the whole mess, both murders, are about money," Lauren said. "Paul only really cared about money, not people," she shivered, despite the blanket. "I guess I always knew that about him. I just didn't want to believe it," she added sadly. She looked at her hands for a minute, then looked up. "If it's about Tisserande money, Paul probably had any information on his laptop." She grimaced lopsidedly, "Paul didn't really have any money but Tisserande's. He always spent every cent he got and then some." Her hand clenched the blanket into a ball.

Max repeated uncertainly, "We'll get it back eventually."

"Eventually might be a long time," Mia said. "And I hate to say it, but Chief White seems very hostile towards Lauren."

"I'll say," Lauren half smiled.

"It's a company laptop, you say? Property of Tisserande?" Mia asked thoughtfully. "The chief left very abruptly. Perhaps he neglected to secure Paul's laptop while he was making his dramatic exit."

Max looked at her with dawning approval. "We can't let valuable company property be left in an empty hotel room. Naturally we will hand it over to the police when they request it."

"Exactly," Mia smiled serenely. "Let me just give Kayla a call to see if she can secure Tisserande's laptop."

Kayla, with a smile way too bright for the hour, delivered the laptop and snacks in just a few minutes.

"Let's see if we can find Paul's financial information. Cynthia told me she made him a different version of the summary of the spreadsheets than I did. It would be nice to know if he was hiding money from me somewhere." Lauren opened the laptop, moving to the center of the sofa while Max and Jeremy crowded close to see. She crunched into an apple slice, entered the master password and started going through Paul's files.

Mia sat patiently, drinking a cup of chamomile tea. Patience was something she'd cultivated long ago. She relaxed in the comfortable chair, half dozing under her cozy blanket, feet propped on a footstool and listened to the others.

Max and Jeremy pointed at the screen, leaning in on Lauren from both sides, "Click on that. Try there. What about that database?" They were both frowning as they went through the computer. Lauren's fingers flew on the keys.

Jeremy exclaimed, "Those don't look like the numbers she gave me either. I can look up the documents, but I'm sure the sales figures for the department stores were much higher last year." He stared at the screen, trying to remember the exact figures he'd seen. "Much higher."

Lauren handed Paul's laptop to Max and pulled up the files on her own computer, frowning as she compared the two.

238

"The sales figures are completely different," Lauren said after a minute. "Melissa was making a lot more money than I would have thought—or I was told. Enough that I would have asked some questions if I'd known about it, I guess." She grimaced. "And Courtney made considerably less in Paul's books than mine. We'll have to make that up to her."

"Melissa made more than me," Jeremy said with a sour grin. "It looks like Melissa got quite a share of Courtney's salary. No wonder she hated Melissa. That's a lot of money." He frowned. "She really needed it, with her mom, too."

"What about the rest of them? How do their salaries compare?" Max asked.

"Well, Paul was making the same salary in both books," Lauren said, confused. "I don't understand. Why would he juggle amounts if he wasn't getting anything out of it?" She looked back and forth at the two screens, frowning. She muttered to herself, "Where is the money?"

"I'm sorry to say, Lauren, that your trustees, at the very least, must have been negligent," Mia said emphatically.

"Uncle Harvey? Tom? I can't imagine them stealing from me." Lauren held back tears.

"I sure can imagine Mandy stealing from you," Jeremy said. "I know she's our second cousin, but she's always been a gold digger. And she was the one who chose Paul as CEO and did most of the hands on meetings. John's not much better. I've never liked either of them." He continued, "Tom's never been around much, always overseas duty. I'm sure whatever paperwork he was sent looked okay." He shook his head. "I don't see Harvey stealing from you either, but..." he trailed off. "Definitely Mandy and John."

"I guess," Lauren said. "But just because I don't like them doesn't mean they're thieves, just that they drive me nuts."

"Maybe Paul gave Mandy money in return for his job," Jeremy suggested.

"What do the books show exactly?" Mia asked curiously.

Lauren stared hopelessly at the screen. "It's going to take a long time to know what's really going on. I'll ask Cynthia in the morning for more details, but it's pretty confusing."

"Take one item and trace it completely. That will give you an idea of what's happening. You'll need a professional audit team to really break it down and trace each number back," Mia suggested. "I can recommend a very thorough auditor Spinel uses."

"Thanks, I don't think I'll be using the last firm again, considering." Lauren scanned the numbers on her screen.

"How about purchases of a particular fabric or item? Pick a basic, like white percale sheeting maybe?" Max said. "Then we know if the changes are on the purchasing orders or sales invoices."

"Good idea," Lauren typed rapidly, with the two men leaned in close to read.

After a moment, she said, "So, looking at our middle of the line percale sheets, we seem to be buying a lot more fabric than the sheets we produce."

"Like how much?" Max asked.

Jeremy pulled up his phone to use the calculator. "Okay, so going with queen sheets for averages, it would be thousands more than we made. Thousands." He frowned. "We'd have to break that down into the different sizes we produced for accuracy, but it's doubtful that could possibly add up any other way. There's not much waste in sheets. They're rectangles."

"So fabric to make thousands of sheets more than you produce," Mia mused.

"Or think we produce," Max said dryly. "Paul was the one who went to all the factories. Maybe he was getting some made under the table."

"I know Uncle Harvey mentioned getting an audit done before I signed the trust dissolution papers. I wonder if he has yet." Lauren tapped the keyboard. "I wish he'd had time to meet with me yesterday like we'd planned, but he said he needed to get all the paperwork finished for today."

"I wonder if that's why Mandy and John showed up at your birthday party tonight," Max said thoughtfully. "They seemed very intent on getting you committed."

"I'll say," Jeremy added. "Who was Paul sitting next to at dinner?"

"Mandy Martin," Mia answered. "They were both huddled rather near the fire." She tried to remember where Paul's drink had been and who had been near it. "I don't think I'd sign any papers until you have a full audit of Tisserande Linens, Lauren."

"Hopefully Uncle Harvey has already done it," Lauren said, looking at the laptop. "But even if he has, he hasn't seen these side by side." She twisted her face. "Okay, I need to send these files to you both, so if Chief White grabs this computer, you can still find out what's going on."

"Good idea," Max said. "I wouldn't be surprised if he wiped the laptop on purpose; he has such a grudge against you. Without evidence or a confession, this could all still be blamed on Melissa or Paul, and you could still be arrested for murder. We really need more."

"I fired the Chief's aunt," Lauren said bitterly. "Only it was Paul who fired her, and I'm the one who wants to reopen the factory and hire people back."

"Hey, everyone in town knows that. No one else blames you. Don't worry." Max grabbed her hand and squeezed hard. "This is all going to work out. We're going to find out who the thieves are with this information. They're probably the murderers too."

"I know," Lauren half smiled at him.

"How can we know which one it is, without having them blame everything on Paul and Melissa?" Mia asked.

"Don't worry, we'll find out," Max reassured her.

"Okay, as soon as you guys have the files, it's time for bed. I know I'm exhausted, so you must be too." Lauren closed the laptop with a snap.

10

A Good Night's Sleep

fter the laptop conference, Lauren took a hot shower, trying to relax as the clean hot water pounded on her skin. She scrubbed her skin raw, trying to wash the day away. It didn't work.

Lying in bed, she tossed and turned. Paul was dead, she thought dully. He wouldn't yell at her, get drunk or chase after women. He wouldn't be accusing her of murder again. Only Chief White would be doing that, in the morning. She stared blankly at the ceiling, eyes gritty with exhaustion and tears.

She couldn't stop the news about Cynthia's betrayal—it must be betrayal with two sets of books that radically different—and Paul's death from circling her mind like a horse on a lunge line. She just couldn't drop it and go to sleep. She really needed to sleep, be at her best tomorrow.

Her mind flitted to her perfect sail with Max. The little sailboat had been a dream to sail. She tried to direct her mind to that, sailing a little sailboat with Max on a breezy sunny day, but the storm clouds moved in and took over the dream.

Paul roared up in a motorboat, rocking the boat wildly, Mandy laughing and pointing at her. Max fell overboard, toppling into the water. He was drowning in the deep water. Paul and Mandy kept circling around and around like sharks as Max slowly disappeared underneath the churning surface, lost forever.

She woke, screaming for help, stopping when she realized what she was doing. She lay still, staring at the ceiling, needing to sleep and dreading the accompanying nightmares. And then she heard a foot carefully step on the wood floor.

Lauren froze.

The careful foot padded on to the soft carpet, almost silent, but now she knew it was there. The blanket weighed her down, trapping her in the soft bed. She wanted to roll over, off the bed, out of danger.

"I know you're awake," Cynthia said calmly. "You were having a bad dream."

Lauren sat up abruptly. "What are you doing here?" Her feet started swinging out of bed. Then she saw the gun in Cynthia's hands and couldn't move if she wanted to.

Cynthia continued in a conversational tone of voice, "I'd planned on you committing suicide after

244

Paul's death." She explained, as if to a dull child, "It would have looked like you'd killed Melissa and Paul, then killed yourself."

Lauren couldn't say a word.

Cynthia looked distastefully at the gun in her hand. "Really, dear, I'm running out of time. You switching rooms so precipitously made it very difficult for me. It took me a while to get the key to this one." Her lips twisted with disapproval. "But then you were always such a selfish girl. You would wake up before I could shoot you. I didn't want you to suffer. If only you'd stayed asleep."

"Why are you doing this?" Lauren asked.

Cynthia waved the gun at Lauren and smiled as she saw her flinch. "For money, of course." She smiled, lips flattening like a snake. "When your parents died, I saw my opportunity for great things. I knew Paul from college and gave him enough information about Mandy to make him a shoo-in for Tisserande's CEO. She had to hire him with what I had on her."

"Mandy?"

Cynthia waved the gun casually. "Yes, dear Mandy has quite a bit she didn't bother to mention about her first husband's unexpected death. Not that she actually murdered the old geezer, but she didn't take him to the hospital when she should have. Negligence at the very least. Jail time for certain. I lived next door, so I saw everything. And I have the video evidence to prove it. The old guy was begging for the emergency room and she just laughed at him," Cynthia gloated. "Such a selfish little bitch."

"Mandy?" Lauren was shocked.

"I could have made life very difficult for her then, but I didn't. And one good turn deserves another." A cruel smile curved across her face. "Instead of going to jail, all she had to do was offer Paul a job. Tisserande paid a lot better than Mandy ever could have. She enjoyed just enough of the little treats to pull her in deeper. And I owned your company from then on, just not in name." Her crocodile smile said it all.

"So Paul did whatever you said?"

"Oh yes, I had evidence on him, too. I knew him in college, like I said." Cynthia shook her head in mock dismay. "Drunks make so many mistakes. And some are fatal to others, you see."

Lauren's mind skittered away from that topic. "Why?"

"Money, as I said."

Lauren said, considering, "So much fabric..."

"Yes, so much fabric." Cynthia's eyes were gleeful. "You bought the fabric to make the sheets I sold, you paid for the factory to make them, even the saleswoman who sold your biggest competitor's sheets on the sales trips you paid for. I was going to leave in two years with all your money, a thriving business and nobody the wiser." She waved the gun at Lauren. "And you were going to spend all the capital I needed access to bring the factory back home, ruining all my plans."

She screwed up her mouth and shook her head at Lauren, "I did ask you not to do that, you know. I tried my very best."

"Why didn't anyone find out?" Lauren said with

shock. "I know the company was audited while it was in trust."

Cynthia laughed in her face. "I chose the auditors and got Mandy to insist on hiring them." She smiled, "Trust me, she knew it was in her best interest to hire my people. Then, I simply bribed them." She smiled again, wider, "Anyone can be bribed, if you know their price."

"And Melissa? Why did you kill her?"

"Well, actually, my dear," Cynthia drew out the endearment like a curse, "I meant to kill you." She shrugged carelessly, "Melissa was so greedy. She would have had to die sooner or later anyway. Her taking the boat just sped it up a little." She looked curiously at Lauren, "I don't know why you care. I did you a favor, killing that bitch."

Lauren had nothing to say.

"And Paul, well, Paul," Cynthia smiled wickedly. "He wasn't much use to me after you started divorce proceedings, for all his posturing about taking the company back. So it was time for him to go." She tilted her head, pleased with herself.

"It wasn't difficult to steal a few of Courtney's migraine medicine. Such a drama queen, constantly complaining about her headaches. And rizatriptan doesn't exactly go well with the alcoholic binge he was on. It was so easy to grind up the tablets and bring them along." Her smile was wide. "Whose idea do you think crashing the party was? I brought him there to murder him," she gloated. "I just tossed the paper spill in the fire after I dropped it in his drink. It was time for him to go." She fingered the gun, bright nail tapping on the trigger. "That way there's only one story. Mine."

She smirked and took a step closer to Lauren. "These old walls are extremely thick. I wonder if I can make that suicide story work after all."

Lauren tensed herself, ready to move.

"Now!" A yell rang out.

Lauren rolled off the bed, fast. Cynthia shot the gun as a hand thrust out from under the bed, pulling her in a hard fall to the floor. Jeremy came out from behind the curtains, pinning Cynthia to the ground while Max grabbed her gun. In a minute, she was lying on the ground like a fallen rag doll.

Mia, coming out from behind the other curtain, was already calmly calling the front desk. "Kayla, please send two security guards to Ms. Tisserande's room immediately."

11

Summing Up

As tired as she was, Lauren couldn't get back to sleep that night. Yawning, she finally gave up the struggle and ventured downstairs in search of coffee.

Bright, streaming sunshine greeted her as she entered the dining room, and she blinked blearily. A cup was gently placed in her hand as she was led to a seat at the edge of the room. Max smiled as he met her eyes. "Couldn't sleep?"

"No," Lauren replied as she took a sip. Sugar and caffeine started working their magic. She breathed in the aroma, slowly waking up.

"It's early yet," he commented. "Don't worry, Cynthia has been under guard all night. I checked. She's not getting away."

"Not this time," Lauren said bitterly. "She's caused a lot of damage." The morning sun streamed over their table. "It's in the past. We can rebuild from here, now that we know."

Max smiled at her and she smiled back. "Now that we know."

They sat there a long time, drinking their coffee in peace.

Mia, well rested as always, strolled down the lobby stairs as Chief White strode in the main entrance. She smiled to herself—this was going to be fun.

He strutted toward Mia, a smug look on his face. "Where is she?" He swiped a paper under her nose, too fast to read. "I have a warrant for the arrest of Mrs. Lauren Baker." He smirked. "I waited all night for the judge to sign this one, but it was worth it."

He barked at her, "Where is she?"

"Ah, Chief White, so nice to see you," Mia said with her best hostess smile. "We have your murderer in custody." She nodded pleasantly at him.

"Yes, I know she's in the hotel," he agreed, slapping the paper hard against his thigh. "And the warrant for her arrest is right here."

"As I reported to the police station this morning, your murderer was caught in the act of attempting to commit another murder."

"What?" he bayed. "That damn judge lives in the

250

middle of nowhere. No one told me." He slapped the order on his leg again. "Well, I'm here now anyway. I want Mrs. Baker off this island where she can't hurt anyone else." He tapped the warrant impatiently.

"And I have it all on video," Mia said with the faintest trace of smugness.

"On video—that's great!" The chief looked at her with approval for the very first time. "Two murders and caught in the act. Mrs. Baker won't ever be coming out after that."

Mia coughed slightly. "Ahem."

He paused impatiently. "Yes?"

"Mrs. Baker was the victim Cynthia Clark tried to kill last night, as I explained to your office. Ms. Clark is the murderer."

"What? Impossible!" He howled at her, disbelieving. "Mrs. Baker is the murderer. She was the only one who wanted Ms. Hathway dead. She killed her husband. She's the murderer, I tell you."

"I assure you, I have a video of Ms. Clark's confession before she tried to shoot Mrs. Baker." Mia kept any traces of her inward glee at his discomfiture off her face. "She admitted to killing Ms. Hathway by mistake. She actually tried to kill Mrs. Baker."

He slapped his warrant hard. "Are you sure? Perhaps she meant something else." He flailed. "Maybe Ms. Clark was getting revenge for the other murders. She may have been close to the victims."

"She shot a gun at Lauren while bragging about her crimes," Mia added with annoyance. "It's lodged in the ceiling of Lauren's hotel room." She continued. "I have video and two more witnesses, Chief White. She confessed to both murders."

"But, but why?" The man was flabbergasted.

"She'd been stealing money from Tisserande Linens for years. Millions." She let that word hang a minute, then continued, "Once she orchestrated the company's production moving overseas, it was very difficult for proper oversight of company affairs." She looked hard at Chief White, letting that sink in. "The first murder, of Ms. Hathway, was an attempted murder of Mrs. Baker." She reprimanded him, "Mrs. Baker has been in grave danger, and completely unprotected by the police force ever since Melissa Hathway's murder."

He looked at the ground, cheeks deflated, like a boy who'd forgotten his homework, "Yes, well..."

She coughed gently. "I did suggest a financial motive, Chief."

"Yes, but, well, there was such a strong personal motive for Mrs. Baker..." he slowly stuttered to a halt, then pointedly tore up the arrest warrant into tiny pieces, throwing them on the front desk. "Where is she?" he snarled.

"Right this way," Mia ushered him down the hallway toward his murderer.

That evening, Mia opened the big French doors and stepped onto the terrace, smiling as she greeted her guests. They all looked a bit shell shocked from the last few days, but on the road to recovery. She smiled at Lauren and said, "I've heard our chefs have a very special dinner planned for us."

"I can't wait," Lauren smiled. She took hold of Max and Jeremy's arms. "Lead me to it."

It was a large group, with all the people she wanted to celebrate with. Courtney was there, as well as Lauren's lawyer, Harvey, who'd been persuaded to actually spend the night on the island. Jake and Blake raced ahead on the path, tossing a ball back and forth as they ran.

Carlos wasn't a chef, but a guest, for this meal. Nick, the bus boy, strutted at his side, savoring the moment. And wonder of wonders, Kayla was off duty and relaxed, at least for her.

Mia directed the group down the little woods path. Tiny lights decorated the trees on their way, looking like fireflies in the branches. Looking up, she saw glimpses of the stars in the deep night sky through the trees. She pointed ahead, to a big white tent set up amongst the trees. A roaring fire stood in the center of the clearing, casting a friendly glow to the area, and making the Maine summer night cozy. It was a scene out of a fairy tale, a magical tent pitched in the middle of the forest.

"What's this?" Lauren asked, delighted.

"The Michauds are cooking for us tonight," Mia explained. "They've found some wonderful ingredients on the island, and they're going to share them with us. A true Maine island meal."

As they stepped into the open tent, Tina waved, "Hello and welcome!" She chopped with fervor at some greens, her softly rounded form wrapped in an apron covered in little lighthouses.

Andrew Michaud boomed, "Welcome to the party!" He was flipping fish on a massive grill, beaming face red from the heat.

Carlos grinned in pride. He'd finally found somewhere for the Michauds to cook. "We use this tent for outdoor wedding dinners. I thought it would be perfect for Andrew and Tina."

Kayla enthused, "I can't wait!" Her blonde hair was extra spiky for the event. She looked like a mischievous forest elf.

One side of the tent was completely open, with the fire cheerfully blazing outside. Colorful flags and lights garlanded the edges, draping to a candlelight chandelier over a massive banquet table. Tiny wildflower bouquets and colorful napkins adorned each place at the long table. The other three sides of the tent had a massive grill, long prep counter and a stove, bounded by a serving table. It was basically an outdoor restaurant, with all the frills of an indoor one.

"Absolute perfection," Mia told Carlos. She thought she'd never seen the couple happier as they bustled around the tent kitchen.

Carlos added, "They'll be coming back to teach a workshop on foraging local foods later in the summer."

"It will be an entirely new cuisine to look

forward to," Andrew rattled some clams on the grill. "Right now, there's the last of the spring and beginning of early summer foods, but I can't wait to find out what's on the island in high summer."

Tina just stirred a bubbling pot, eyes dreamy with the thought of gourmet meals from the Maine summer.

"That sounds wonderful!" Lauren said. "Sign me up. I can't wait to find out more about what's delicious in my own backyard."

"Absolutely," Max said, putting his arm around Lauren. "And the way she's going to be working us, Jeremy and I will both need a break in the great outdoors."

"So the factory is going ahead as planned?" Mia asked.

"Definitely," Lauren told her, leaning into Max's arm. "I'm more determined than ever to build it—now that I know those jobs never had to be lost in the first place. It was all Paul and Cynthia's greed."

Harvey coughed, "I cannot believe," he shook his head and continued, "I just cannot believe that a reputable firm of accountants would have lied to us, yes, lied to us multiple times in a professional audit." He shook his head again. "It beggars belief."

"Not so reputable a firm now," Jeremy added. "I think we'll be going with Mia's suggestion of an honest one."

Harvey said, "At least, with Paul's unfortunate death occurring while intestate, we've been able to recover most of the money he had stolen. His laptop pointed us to the accounts he'd placed it in." His dry cough punctuated that with, "Of course, the money Cynthia stole has still to be recovered, but we have found a great deal of it so far. It is mostly tied up in her rival linen company. We just have to trace it."

"It's hard to believe those two were able to do so much damage with no one noticing," Courtney added in a soft voice.

Harvey coughed, "Mea culpa, I'm afraid." He sighed, "With Mandy and John wishing to work directly with Paul and Cynthia, I'm afraid I let them. I thought the accountants would keep them honest. I never dreamed they were all dishonest." He looked sorrowfully at Lauren, "I trusted them to do their share of the work. A grave oversight on my part."

Lauren reached her arms around the little lawyer. "Uncle Harvey, I didn't dream they were stealing. I'm not surprised you believed the auditors. After all, I even married Paul," she shuddered slightly.

He patted her back once, awkwardly. "Thank you, my dear."

"I'm just glad the whole nightmare is over. You've already got most of the money back and the rest will be cleaned up soon. And Cynthia completely broke down when she saw the video of her confessing to murder while attempting another. Mine." Lauren's mouth twisted. "She'll spend a very long time in jail."

"Thank goodness," Mia said.

Nick broke in, "She must have been the lady Mr. Baker was arguing with that night in the library."

"I think you're right, Nick," Mia agreed. "She

must have known she'd have to kill him before he got a divorce."

Harvey added, "And quickly, before Lauren signed her trust paperwork. That way it would be an estate the crooked accountants could deal with, not an unknown firm of accountants."

"And the new factory would be stopped, so they wouldn't lose access to the capital," Max said.

"I can't believe she'd set up another company, using our money," Jeremy said. "Who thinks of that? She even used Melissa as her salesperson. No wonder her numbers always seemed off for the amount of time she spent on the road."

Courtney said softly, "I remember one sales trip we took, Melissa disappeared for a very long time, half the day." She made a face, "I thought she'd found some guy, and I told her off for wasting time. It turns out she was working after all, just for Cynthia's company, not Tisserande." She shrugged a little, delicately holding her hands up. "Who knew?" She laughed sardonically, "That was the last sales trip we made together, now that I think of it."

Jeremy smiled at her, "I doubt they wanted you to find out what they were up to." He put his arm around her shoulders.

She smiled up at him, her big brown eyes luminous in the soft light. "I wanted to keep my job because of my mom, you know. So I tried not to notice much. I thought they were just stealing for Melissa from the sales team, not the company."

"How could you have known?" Jeremy hugged

her tighter.

Mia thought to herself, Jeremy and Courtney would make a cute couple, now that Jeremy realized he had a pretty special girl right next to him, all along. Mia saw him smiling down at her with gentle love.

Max had known all along how special Lauren was, Mia thought. After Lauren recovered from the breakup of her terrible marriage, they could start sharing their lives together. Mia smiled to herself and breathed in the wonderful smells of the Michaud's gourmet cooking.

"Some nibbles to start," Tina called, sliding a tray onto the serving counter.

Oysters on a half shell didn't wait for long. Mia squeezed a tiny bit of lemon onto hers and let the briny oyster slide into her mouth. "Delicious."

Tina followed with delicate pastries filled with greens and goat cheese. "Lambs quarters," she explained. "They taste a lot like spinach, but are better fresh when you pick them yourself."

Jake wolfed the three he'd grabbed down then looked at the empty tray with dismay. "Those were great. Don't you have any more?"

"Just wait for what's next," Tina told him, glancing back at the stove. Fern fiddleheads filled the saucepan and chowder bubbled.

"Chanterelles?" Mia asked hopefully.

"Wait and see." With a smile, Tina turned back to the stove.

Mia poured a glass of champagne for herself, then more for all who came. As she slowly sipped the dry bubbles, she tried to see what Andrew was grilling. Several split lobsters lay on the grill, steaming. Andrew was in constant motion, repositioning them for the optimal amount of charring heat.

She looked at the happy group around her, chattering and laughing in the firelight. Mia held up her glass in a toast, shimmering in the firelight. "To the best Maine summer yet."

Ms. Mia Murder Mysteries

Lighthearted and Fun Mysteries
with Satisfying Conclusions.

A luxurious private island paradise, with palm trees and white sand beaches, sets the stage for this classic cozy mystery.

A priceless discovery. A glamorous desert resort. And an unexpected mystery... At the Desert Sunrise Resort, Ms. Mia is preparing to host a dazzling exhibit featuring an ancient flute unearthed on the property.

In a sun-drenched tropical paradise, Ms. Mia chases a vanishing corpse and a cunning killer in this delightful cozy murder mystery.

An Italian villa vacation turns deadly—Ms. Mia unmasks a cunning poisoner in this lighthearted cozy murder mystery.

Amid sultry jazz, glittering facades, and long-buried secrets, Ms. Mia untangles a dangerous web of money, loyalty, and betrayal. With wit, charm and a glass of champagne, can Ms. Mia catch the villain before they strike again?

Coming in Summer 2026: Ms. Mia and Murder at Bluegrass Run

J ennifer Branch writes classic mysteries set in
glamorous destinations.

Her Ms. Mia Murder Mysteries follow an
elegant amateur sleuth as she uncovers secrets and
solves murders at luxurious resorts around the world—
from Georgia's Sea Islands and remote Maine retreats
to sunlit deserts, tropical islands, and historic
European villas.

Often compared to a modern Miss Marple with
champagne, the series blends traditional puzzle-
solving, gentle humor, and richly drawn settings for
readers who enjoy classic whodunits with a strong
sense of place.

A lifelong landscape painter, Jennifer brings an
artist's eye to every setting. She lives in Northwest
Georgia with her husband, their sons, and two
adventurous dogs.

Discover more Ms. Mia mysteries, exclusive art,
and behind-the-scenes insights at
www.JenniferBranch.com.

www.ingramcontent.com/pod-product-compliance
Lightning Source LLC
Chambersburg PA
CBHW020913130726
47904CB00006BA/1912